I am not falling in love.

I am never going to fall in love again. But Kate fell asleep dreaming herself into Mark's arms, and woke next morning knowing that the chill of daylight was not cooling the fever in her blood. So she was no different from the other women who simpered when they met him. Her advantage was that for a little while they would be living together . . .

Dear Reader

In this year of European unity, July sees the launch in hardback (September paperback) of an intriguing new series—contemporary romances by your favourite Mills & Boon authors, but with a distinctly European flavour. Look out for the special cover of a love story every month set in one of the twelve EC countries, which will take you on a fascinating journey to see the sights, life and romance, Continental style.

Vive l'amour in 1992—who do *you* think is Europe's sexiest hero?

The Editor

Jane Donnelly began earning her living as a writer as a teenage reporter. When she married the editor of the newspaper she freelanced for women's mags for a while, and wrote her first Mills & Boon romance as a hard-up single parent. Now she lives in a roses-round-the-door cottage near Stratford-on-Avon, with her daughter, four dogs and assorted rescued animals. Besides writing she enjoys travelling, swimming, walking and the company of friends.

Recent titles by the same author:

ONCE A CHEAT

THE TRESPASSER

BY

JANE DONNELLY

MILLS & BOON LIMITED
ETON HOUSE   18-24 PARADISE ROAD
RICHMOND   SURREY   TW9 1SR

First published in Great Britain 1992
by Mills & Boon Limited

© Jane Donnelly 1992

Australian copyright 1992
Philippine copyright 1992
This edition 1992

ISBN 0 263 77652 2

Set in Times Roman 11 on 11½ pt.
01-9208-50583 C

Made and printed in Great Britain

CHAPTER ONE

SHE remembered the shape of it. The irregular line of the squat tower in the mouth of the bay. Today the sea and the sky were a leaden grey and there were no boats out there, nobody else on this wind-swept sea-front.

It was the end of October now. It had been summer then, although she remembered shivering, gripping the iron rail that topped the harbour wall, looking across at the tower and wishing she could hide inside because it seemed such a wonderfully safe hiding place.

She had wondered what it was like in there, and she was still wondering. The causeway was clear, the wide flat stones led across the shore straight for the tower, and she was stiff with a slight headache after all those hours on the road. This was good fresh air she was breathing, but going by the massing clouds it could be raining before long, so she might as well take some exercise before she booked into a guesthouse.

She buttoned up her black trenchcoat, pulled up her collar and tucked her hair under a black felt hat. She picked up a shoulder bag, locked the door of the red Mini, then went round to get her briefcase from the boot.

There was no real need to take the briefcase with her. There was not a soul in sight, and the very few cars seemed parked and empty. But Alan had said,

'Promise you'll never be parted from it,' and she had joked,

'I solemnly swear that wherever it goes, I will go.'

In a way it was the tower that had brought her here. Reading the 'For Sale, Genuine Martello Tower' notice in a Sunday paper. She had thought Alan wanted her with him on the American trip, until he had explained that the schedule was a hundred per cent business and he was expected alone. Turning up with a blonde knockout of a girl, guaranteed to distract him and everyone else, would be a black mark against him.

She had fixed her time off, jumping the gun, announcing gleefully, 'I'm coming too!' and he had been so concerned and so apologetic that she had fallen over herself to assure him it didn't matter, she didn't mind. It was just that she'd had this time owing. She would still take it, she could do with a break, and off-season and what with the weather being so miserable she should have no problem getting in anywhere.

She had picked up a paper and seen the advert, and said, 'We went there on holiday when I was a child. I might go back and take another look. It was a pretty place.'

She had made herself sound enthusiastic. For him, and for anybody who had presumed she would be going with Alan Foster although she had never actually said that.

'Aren't you going with Alan, then?' Jenny had asked. 'Whyever not?' Jenny Blair had big brown eyes that always seemed on the lookout for something mournful, and Kate said briskly,

'No, he's away on high-pressure business, so I'll just be loafing around for a few days.'

Jenny had a kind heart and the last thing Kate wanted was anybody suspecting she was disappointed. Sympathy was something she could always do without, and no one need feel sorry for Kate Kershaw who was smart and sassy and quite successful. With the long-legged elegance and cool beauty of a fashion model.

She had been told that often enough, but it was not until Alan said she was beautiful that she had finally believed that she was.

How big the tower seemed as you came closer. Halfway across the causeway it began to loom against the skyline, and when she stepped on to the little rocky island and looked up at the walls it seemed impregnable, as it must have been when cannon covered the open sea and armed men peered out of the narrow windows and down from the battlements.

Time had battered it, but it was still massively impressive, and now there was a way in. A flight of stone steps led to the entrance that once had been bricked up, with only the remains of a rusted ladder adhering to the walls, and no way a child could climb up there.

Kate had walked carefully over the wet stones and looked out for sea-moss on the rocks, but she was so thrilled to see the steps that she slithered hurrying towards them and getting up to the door.

The door seemed old, but it could be a reproduction. The tower had been advertised as an attractive and unusual home after extensive renovation. The door was heavy and dark, studded and hinged in black iron, and there was no knocker or bell.

She hammered with her fist and called, 'Hello!' but the sounds she made were lost on the wind. When nobody answered she banged again, and then, as she pushed it, the door swung gently ajar.

She was still shouting, 'Hello, anyone home?' and now her raised voice echoed back from the rounded walls of the enormous room. The walls were painted white, the granite floor slabs had been sandblasted and polished, and a large black dog came loping purposefully towards her.

'Down, boy!' she croaked, and at the same time a man called,

'If you're here to view, come on up.'

She skirted the dog and there were stone steps behind an archway, narrow and curving and blocked almost entirely by the man, who turned and went ahead of her, waiting for her to join him on the first landing.

She didn't take to him on sight. For no good reason, as she climbed the last two steps and came face to face with him, a frown puckered her brow and she almost said, 'I'm not a buyer, you'd be wasting your time showing me round.' Although she really wanted to see what somebody had made of the tower.

He was tall, broad-shouldered but thinnish, with very dark hair and thick eyebrows, and piercingly direct eyes that looked as if they never blinked.

Her first impression was, you're an awkward customer. Then he smiled and said, 'This way, madam,' and she smiled back because it was an attractive grin, which did nothing to change her mind about him.

The advert was right. The tower was something different in the way of homes, but you could have lived in it very comfortably. Conversion had produced five bedrooms, two bathrooms, and a big living-room on the upper storeys; and although Kate couldn't have met the purchase price even with a couple of noughts knocked off she let her imagination roam.

It was furnished but stark, and it would be fun to own somewhere like this and have money to spend on it. You might not need a fortune, there were auctions and junk shops. All you would really need would be a mortgage that no one was going to advance on her salary.

Her guide didn't say much. He opened doors and let her look in or step in without pointing out the obvious, like, 'This is another bathroom,' or 'The views are spectacular.'

She could almost have been alone, but she was very conscious of him standing there, watching her with a faintly weary air, as if she were the latest in a long line of sightseers.

Well, she was sightseeing, but she wasn't causing all that much trouble, and she flashed him the occasional smile. He was barefoot, in jeans and a grey rollneck sweater, and he could have done with a shave. She wondered if he was the caretaker and if she ought to tip him before she left.

Now they were back where they had started, in the pleasant living-room with its ethnic rugs and deep comfortable chairs. This was the cosiest spot too, some rooms were arctic, but in here the dog sprawled in front of an ornate black cast-iron stove that gave out a welcoming heat. And Kate crossed to it, holding out her hands for a final warm-up.

'Nice stove,' she said.

'Temperamental. It needs replacing.'

This was the first snag he had mentioned, but he hadn't given a sales pitch either, and she asked, 'Are you the owner?'

'Yes.'

Her lips twitched. 'I was wondering if I ought to tip you for showing me around.'

'There's an idea.'

She laughed. 'Forget it. Owning a place like this, you could afford to be tipping me.'

'Well, how about a cup of coffee on the house?'

'Well, thank you,' she said, 'I'd like that very much,' and she was surprised at how eager she was to stay a little longer.

Of course, that was because she was fascinated by the tower. At times she got the sort of tingle she was getting now, as if she was tuning in to something exciting. It was a kind of sixth sense, and very useful in her line of business.

The kitchen was downstairs, through another archway. The dog followed the man and Kate wandered around rubbernecking. She hadn't noticed much while she was dodging the dog, but now she saw the big scrubbed-top old table with the oil lamp in the centre, the dresser, the hatstand, waterproofs and anoraks hanging and wellie boots piled beneath.

She stood at a window looking out to sea. On the rock shelf below the big gun would have stood, primed and ready for Napoleon's invasion that never came. Cannon balls would be piled high, and she could imagine the scurrying figures, hear the boom and smell the cordite.

She *could* smell smoke, sharp and acrid, and she turned, sniffing the air and freezing in horror as she saw the grey cloud billowing from the staircase. Then she screamed, 'Fire!' and leapt into action, and the man grabbed her arm just before she reached the archway.

'Let go of me! I left my briefcase up there!' She tore herself loose so violently that she cracked her head back against the wall and stars danced in front of her eyes.

He stood, barring her way, smoke drifting lazily past him, telling her, 'It isn't fire, it's smoke.'

'No smoke without fire,' she quoted hoarsely.

'This is the exception. That smoke blows black in windy weather. Usually it's only the one great belch.' It was thinning and no more seemed to be coming. 'I'll get it for you,' he said.

'Are you sure?'

In that split second she had visualised a spark on the cushion where she had placed the briefcase and everything swooshing up like tinder. Her heart was still hammering, and so was the back of her head where she had hit the wall.

When he brought her the briefcase she almost grabbed it from him, babbling her thanks, and then he opened the door wide to let out the smoke. There was hardly any sign of it now, just the smell lingered. 'What kind of merchandise are you carrying?' he asked.

She had panicked, and that wasn't like her. 'It's notes for a book.'

'Not the latest Ministry of Defence leak?' He had a deep voice, slow and amused, and she had made rather an idiot of herself.

She quipped back, 'Nothing even remotely illegal.'

'You look the part for a spy. The woman in black. And that's a very suspicious hat.'

She had knocked her hat forward so that the brim shadowed her eyes, and she straightened it now. 'The one and only manuscript,' she explained.

'You're a writer?'

'Yes.'

She was a journalist on local radio, but Alan's book was out of her league. It was special and she was thrilled to be typing it for him, helping him, but she was not discussing that with a stranger.

'Take a seat.' He pulled out one of the rush-seated ladder-backed chairs pushed up to the table, and she slumped a little. She had nearly knocked herself out. There was probably a lump rising on the back of her head right now, but she wasn't making a fuss here. She would ask for some aspirins where she booked in for the night.

'Milk and sugar?' he called.

'Nearly black. No sugar. Thank you.'

She got a red mug. He sat opposite with a blue-ringed one and she thought woozily that she would have expected at least a matching pair.

'Are you all right?' She might be pale and she had been right, he didn't blink. The piercing eyes looked straight at her and she looked down into her coffee as if meeting his gaze would be taking on a challenge.

'I will be when I've drunk this.' It was too hot to swallow more than a sip at a time. She managed a couple of gulps. 'That's better.' But she still didn't look at him. 'I must be on my way. What time does the tide start coming in?'

'About now.'

'Then I must go.' She managed a very little more before she stood up and he asked,

'Are you staying locally?'

'Yes, I've just arrived. Could you recommend anywhere? I'll probably be here for two weeks, working on this.' She picked up the briefcase. 'I was going to say somewhere quiet, but everywhere seems that. I didn't see much sign of life.'

She reached the door and was talking to him over her shoulder. When he said, 'I could recommend here,' she spun round.

'But that would be splendid!' The advert hadn't mentioned it, but the tower was ideally situated and designed for holiday lets. 'I didn't realise you took in tourists. Do you have anyone else staying?'

'Not at the moment—the season's over. It's self-catering, but the rooms are there, you're welcome to one.'

She had come here because she couldn't think of anywhere else she much wanted to go. The choice had been as haphazard as picking a name out of a hat, but she had done well. It must be her consolation prize for not going with Alan. 'Oh, I'll take it,' she said gaily, and for the first time she knew that she was going to enjoy herself. 'I'll get my bag.'

'Where is it?'

'In the red car.' She pointed to the small splash of colour on the drab sea-front. By now everything else seemed to be in varying shades of grey. The clouds were lower and darker and the black-grey sea was already lapping over the stones of the causeway.

'Give me the keys,' he said.

'My suitcase is in the boot. How fast does the tide come in? You're not going to get cut off, are you?'

'No,' and she supposed that was as stupid as being asked if she knew her way around the town where she lived and worked. But she stood in the doorway watching him walk with the dog towards the deserted beach.

Soon it would be dark as late afternoon turned into night, and the wind had dropped suddenly, leaving a heavy stillness in the air. In the few minutes it took for them to start walking back the sea was swirling over the causeway until, on the last stretch, the man was wading and the dog was doing a paddling stroke.

As they reached the rock and began to come up the steps she asked, 'Do you lose many lodgers this way?'

'Tide times are printed loud and clear and they're all briefed until they can recite them in their sleep,' he told her.

'You'd better brief me.'

'Count on it. I'll show you your room.'

It was high in the tower with two narrow windows overlooking the open sea. He put her suitcase down and brought her sheets and pillowcases. 'Have you eaten?' he asked.

'Well, no.' She had expected a meal where she stayed, but if it was self-catering here...

'Join me, in half an hour?'

'Thank you.'

He left her to make her own bed, and she took off her hat and coat and went along to a bathroom and washed the travel grime away. Then she opened her case and took out Alan's photograph, kissed it and placed it on the table by the bed, so that he was with her as she shook out and tucked in sheets, topping them with the duvet, and then flopping down, lowering her head gingerly on to the pillows.

She smiled at Alan with sleepy eyes, and she always felt that this photograph smiled back. It was a studio study, and when it appeared on his election leaflets it was going to be a vote-winner, because as well as his natural good looks this brought out the caring qualities. Those were the eyes of a man you could trust. The mouth was firm and the jawline was strong.

The selection committee would be crazy if they didn't choose him as their candidate, and the voters would be blind if they didn't elect him. Alan Foster was a man who knew where he was going, and Kate Kershaw was going with him. He told her that often, and she looked into his eyes and saw her future and knew that she was the luckiest girl in the world.

She was missing him now, wishing he was with her, or she with him, but as well as his political ambitions there was a family business he helped to run; and the American market was one of the reasons the Fosters were rich and Alan was an eligible bachelor on every count. But Kate loved him just for himself, the way he loved her.

And although she hadn't eaten for hours she would have preferred to stay where she was, dozing and dreaming of Alan, instead of going down and eating a meal with a stranger with whom she probably had not a thing in common.

'I don't even know his name,' she told Alan's photograph. 'But I know you wouldn't like him, and you're a very good judge of character.'

She got off the bed reluctantly, combed her hair and applied token lipstick. Blow the rest. She was on holiday and out to impress no one. When she had looked into the bedrooms earlier it had been cold, but now the temperature was warming up and she thought she heard a distant rumble of thunder. There could be a storm before the night was out, but if there was this was the place to be, a fortress built to withstand a bombardment where lightning would never strike you.

He called her from the open door of the living-room. He had shaved and he was now wearing trainers, but he still looked tough and fairly rough. In there a table was laid. The fire glowed behind the bars, but now Kate knew what that stove could do in the way of blow-back she was keeping her distance. Smoke that could reach downstairs would nearly asphyxiate you if you got the full blast.

She asked, 'How do your guests react to little Vesuvius here?' and he shrugged,

'They're summer trade. Usually I use Calor gas heating. I only light the stove for myself, and it doesn't happen often. Does it make you nervous?'

'Not now I know what it is.' The stove sat squarely on bulbous feet, a wide pipe funnelled into an air duct. 'It's grinning,' she said. 'The damn thing's laughing at me!' and he laughed with her, although it was a silly joke.

The meal was simple, the main course a tureen of thick vegetable soup. It was hot and she was hungry, and when she took her first mouthful she said, 'Congratulations to the chef.'

'We'll drop them a line. The address is on the tins.'

'You don't cook for the customers?'

'No.'

'You live here, in the tower?' She asked personal questions for a living, so they tripped naturally off her tongue.

'Sometimes,' he said.

'Do you do anything else, besides run this place?'

She liked to know about folk she met, and because she was young and attractive even those she chatted up casually were usually flattered and willing to tell her a great deal.

She was leaning towards him, eyes bright, lips curved, but for a moment she thought he was going to tell her to mind her own business. Then he said, 'I'm a photographer,' and that led to her next question.

'Is that your shop in the High Street?'

'Yes.'

'I noticed it while I was driving through.' She recalled the name overhead, 'T. Brandon.'

'You don't miss much.' In case he meant she should have been watching the road she defended herself,

'There was hardly anything about and I was looking for somewhere to stay, only most of them had ''No Vacancies'' up. What does the T stand for?'

'Thaddeus.'

She yelped before she could stop herself, then clapped a hand across her mouth. 'Sorry, but however do you cope with that?'

'You can get used to anything.' He didn't seem bothered. 'And you are?'

'Kate Kershaw.'

'Kate.' He sounded as if he was measuring it against her, but there wasn't much you could say about a name like Kate. 'A good Shakespearean name,' he said.

'*The Taming of the Shrew* is not my favourite play.' The bread rolls seemed freshly baked. She had passed a pastry shop too. She spread butter and sighed, 'The things that girl went through!'

'Petruchio must have had something going or she wouldn't have stood for it,' he said.

'Like what?'

'Rampant sex appeal?' he suggested, and she thought, You're not short of that, or why should I feel that reaching over the soup bowls and brushing your hand might be like touching a live wire? She pretended to sigh again.

'And she was such a well-brought-up girl. Do you have a family, by the way?'

'No. Do you?'

'No.' He glanced at her left hand and she held it up, spreading her long slim fingers with their pearl pink nails. 'No family and no ring.'

'That means nothing,' he said, and she must have been looking smug, because all her ringless finger did mean was that the commitment between herself and Alan was something of a secret for now. They had this superstition that they would hold back the announcement until he *was* a prospective MP. Then at the party to celebrate his selection as candidate, they would announce their engagement, and Kate would be wearing the antique pearl and emerald ring that had belonged to his grandmother.

He had already put it on her finger and it was a perfect fit, and he said, 'If they don't want me we won't be waiting until I get shortlisted again.'

'Of course they'll choose you,' she'd promised him. 'They'll be lucky to get you. And now I know how it looks and feels I can feel your ring on my finger even if nobody else can see it. Put it away now.' She had handed it back with a little pang, but very soon she would be wearing it forever.

'So why isn't he with you?' Thaddeus asked.

'Business.'

'He lets you wander off on your own?'

'I'm a big girl, I do a lot of wandering. I'm a radio reporter.'

'Reporting what?'

She liked talking about her work, doing interviews of local interest. There were often celebrities, but most of them were ordinary people with a story to tell. Her enthusiasm bubbled as she recounted some of her brighter, lighter moments.

He listened and asked questions and laughed at the jokes and seemed really interested, and it was all very pleasant indeed.

There was cheese and fruit following the soup, an untidy table as though she had dropped in unexpectedly on a friend. Kate couldn't have said when she started feeling that way, but after a while she was almost believing that she had known him long enough to have done this before, because it seemed so familiar. Including the gently snoring dog and the old stove.

A bottle of red wine was helping her relax, and by the time she had kicked off her shoes under the table she knew what he had paid for the tower five years ago, when it was a ruin going cheap.

Restoring it with the help of friends must have been an almighty slog, but exciting, and she said fervently, 'Oh, I wish I'd been around to lend a hand!' Her hands, peeling a peach, looked too pampered for a building site, and she said, 'In a good tough pair of industrial gloves.'

'I wish you had been here,' he told her.

His job didn't seem to matter to him the way her work could obsess her. His father had been the local photographer and the son was left with the shop, and she asked, 'You enjoy it?'

'Sometimes.'

'Only sometimes?' That was half-hearted, and she wondered, 'Then why don't you do something else?'

'I often ask myself that.' He poured more wine for them both, and next thing they were discussing television programmes, what she watched, what she turned off. She wasn't sure how they got on to that, but like all the talking it was easy and she seemed to be doing most of it.

When she looked at her watch she was surprised how late it was. She thought at first that the watch was playing up, but the second hand ticked steadily and their plates held the remains of their meal. The wine bottle was empty and the fire was down to embers.

Kate offered to help clear the table, but he said, 'Start washing up tomorrow, you're a guest to-night,' and that was sensible. Until she knew her way around the kitchen and the cupboards she wouldn't know where to put anything, so she said, 'Thank you, it was a lovely meal.'

She stroked the dog and went up the narrow stairs to her room, musing on the fact that it might have been a very ordinary meal so far as the food went, but she had often eaten better and enjoyed herself less.

It had to be because she was so thrilled at getting herself booked in here. There was a table under the window where she could put her typewriter tomorrow. She would ask if she could bring up a chair from downstairs because the only seat was a sagging armchair. Tomorrow she would start work, and Alan would be pleased if he knew what a perfect workplace she had found.

Suddenly she was so tired that she almost fell into bed, wincing as her head hit the pillow. She had forgotten the bump, which was a small tender spot, and she lay listening to the sea. The thickness of the walls muted it to murmuring sighs, and what light there was filtering through the windows filled the room with shadows.

After a few minutes she could make out Alan's face, and that was all she needed to see. He had grey eyes, steady and steadfast, and she loved him very much. Thaddeus's eyes were black as tar, and nobody in their right mind would vote for him.

She smiled at Alan's photograph, and heard the thunder again. It had been rumbling around for hours, but she had hardly noticed it while they were talking and it wasn't troubling her now. It was still far away, and she wriggled between the sheets and was soon sleeping soundly.

She woke to the clash of cymbals. Well, that was how it sounded—a deafening crash right on her eardrums that jerked her upright. She must have been dead to the world, burrowed under the duvet and the pillows, but she was awake now, with the start of a raging headache.

The lightning that had arrived with the thunder was still leaping around the room in blue flashes, like laser beams at a demented rock concert.

Kate felt awful. The storm or the wine or the bang on her head, or a combination of all three, was pounding a pulse in the base of her skull, and no way was she getting to sleep again in this state.

She lurched to a window, opening it, but no air came in, and the sky was a weirdly livid green and indigo. She could have gone back to bed and pulled the duvet over her head, but that would have blown her headache into a full-scale migraine.

She pressed her throbbing forehead against an iron bar across the window, and in the pause between lightning flashes she saw a glow from below. From the living-room. Thaddeus might still be up, and failing painkillers he might supply a cup of tea.

She grabbed her navy blue robe and shut her eyes and ears to the next flash and crash. She was not phobic about storms, although this was a humdinger, but she hoped he was up and the light hadn't been left on because she was feeling fragile and vulnerable and in need of company.

At least the lights hadn't failed. She would have expected the storm to play havoc with the power lines. There was probably a generator, but she didn't risk pressing switches, and she got down the stairs by the light from windows and the open door of the living-room.

Only a lamp burned in there. Thaddeus was pacing the room, striding up and down like a man in a cage, and it was the dog who saw her standing in the doorway. When the dog got up the man looked round, and it was as though the door had been slammed in her face.

She hardly recognised him. He looked grim and gaunt and ten years older, and she was intruding at the worst possible time. She stammered, 'I'm sorry,' and turned to get away, but before she reached the stairs he asked,

'What can I do for you?'

His voice was steady and he was almost smiling, the right tone and expression for reassuring a nervous guest who had woken in a spectacular thunderstorm, and she babbled, 'The storm woke me, and I don't know whether it's the air pressure or the wine, but I'm getting a thumping headache; and I saw a light on in here, and if you could possibly provide a couple of aspirins it might just save my life.'

'Did you look in a bathroom cabinet?'

'Sorry, no. I just staggered down.'

'Come and sit down and I'll see what I can find.'

She went into the room. The table was cleared, but he was still fully dressed, so she couldn't have been asleep for long, and as soon as he came back she would go back to her room.

He had not expected her to come barging in on him again. They had had a cheerful meal together, but they were only acquaintances, and that first glance, when he saw her in the doorway, had been almost savagely aggressive, although it was immediately controlled. Whatever was haunting him—money problems, as he was selling the tower? Woman trouble?—Kate knew instinctively that she would be wise to leave well alone.

He brought her a glass of water and a bottle with half a dozen paracetamols, and she tipped out two of the tablets and got them down. 'Thank you,' she said.

'All part of the service.'

There was a few seconds' space now between the lightning and the thunder peal, and she asked, 'How long has it been going on?'

'Like this? Half an hour or so.'

'It's only just woken me, I must have been deep asleep. What time is it?'

'Three o'clock.'

She had expected around midnight at the latest. She quoted the old wives' saying, 'Three o'clock, the dying hour.'

'The time of nightmares.'

She was facing him, holding the glass in both hands. 'Everything looks brighter in the morning,' she said.

'Is that your experience?'

'I think so.' She couldn't help. She didn't know what was wrong, and it was no concern of hers. 'But I do know that it's a lucky one who hasn't been hammered by life,' she said.

'And what was the worst thing that's happened to you?'

He spoke quietly, and she blurted without giving herself time to consider what she was saying, 'Being jilted at the altar. There have been other black spots, of course, and that was a long time ago, but I guess it was one of the worst.'

Nobody ever talked about it now. It was almost forgotten, and Kate was so very thankful that she had never married Philip. 'What *is* the matter?' she asked, and he said,

'Nothing that you or I can do a blind thing about. But thank you.'

He took the glass from her and put it down. Then he tilted her chin so that she was looking up at him, smoothed the damp tendrils of hair back from her forehead and told her, 'Whoever he was, you had a lucky escape. The man was certifiable!'

That made her smile, as another flash of lightning burst around them so brilliant that it almost blinded her.

She was not thinking clearly, she was hardly thinking at all. It was a moment of pure sensation, because she was totally in love with Alan. Alan was her mate and her lover for life. But while the thunder rolled and she stayed still and quiet and pressed against this man she found herself wondering, just fantasising, of course, how lovemaking would be with him.

She lingered no longer. Her head was still thumping, but the pain was bearable, and she moved away, trying to smile. 'I woke for the grand finale, didn't I? Well, now I'll go back to bed and wait for the pills to work.'

'See you in the morning,' he said.

'Try to get some rest yourself.' He couldn't have been to bed at all, and she wondered if the storm had triggered his 'time of nightmares'.

This was a wild coastline, there must have been shipwrecks here, tragedies, but whatever was torturing him she must not pry again, and she shivered in her bed as if she had brushed against something dark and dangerous.

She reached out for Alan's photograph and put it on her pillow beside her, but for once her imagination failed to conjure up the feel of his arms around her and his warm body encircling hers.

Listening to the storm she felt cold and lonely. With encouragement Thaddeus would probably have come back to her room with her, but you didn't take chances with strangers these days. Not that she ever had, and she really knew nothing about him.

For all she knew, he might not care for the risks of casual sex either. He might have said no, thanks, she might still be lying here alone and feeling much worse than she did now.

But the idea of her propositioning him, or any man but Alan, was so absurd that she had to laugh.

She put the photograph back on the table and, as the storm played itself out, the painkillers soothed and dulled her nervous system until she went slowly drifting down into a painless, dreamless sleep.

CHAPTER TWO

KATE lay still for a few minutes after she woke, listening to the shrill cries of seagulls and then to the barking of the dog.

It was still raining. There were none of the clear bright skies that often followed a bad storm. This sky looked sullen, and although the rain was hardly a downpour it was enough to spoil the day.

It was a shame. She had planned to start work on Alan's book, but it would have been good to wake to sunshine and stroll along the beach first, getting the benefit of some sea air.

The living-room was empty this morning, and she found the man and the dog down in the kitchen. 'Morning, both,' she said.

'Good morning, Kate. Tea or coffee?'

'Coffee, please.' The scrubbed-top table was laid for two, so they seemed to be breakfasting together, but she really could not go on calling him Thaddeus. Not without smiling. 'Do you have another name?' she asked.

'Mark.'

'You don't use Thaddeus?'

'No.' Well, who would?

'Thank goodness for that!' she said. 'Is this chair for me?'

'Of course, but if you're expecting a cooked breakfast you can get it yourself. Fruit, cereal, toast is what I run to.'

'Me too. We didn't get round to discussing terms
last night—what do you charge?'

It was reasonable, and she was sorry he was
selling. She might have come here again when she
was not alone, although perhaps the set-up was
rather rugged for Alan. She had never seen him
prepare a meal.

Mark produced toast and there was butter and
honey, and they ate without talking much, as
though they had known each other long enough to
be past the need for polite conversation.

After last night, when she had been trembling
and nearly naked in his arms, they were hardly
strangers. It had been only a gesture of comfort on
his part, but, licking a crumb of toast from the
corner of her mouth, she remembered the rough
wool of his sweater against her lips and a strange
little thrill ran down her spine.

She was on her second cup of coffee when she
asked, 'Have we met before?'

'No.'

She met so many people in her work and socially,
and she smiled, 'It must have been another man.'

'There are a lot of us about,' he said, but that
made her shake her head.

Breakfast over, she put on her coat to fetch her
typewriter from the car and stood sighing in the
doorway. 'I might as well be working, it's a dreary
day.'

'A drop of water won't melt you.'

He had the dog at his heels, and she said, 'I know
that,' and found herself off the causeway, walking
with them across the hard shining sands. Rain came
down in a cool mist, and the wind buffeted her,
making her face tingle, lifting and tangling her hair.

It was quite exhilarating, blowing all the cobwebs from her mind.

The dog raced after a stick of driftwood it had found, bringing it back and circling Mark in an ecstatic expectant dance, then tearing away again. There was no one else on the shore. The great bounding animal had a playground all to himself. 'What's his name?' she asked.

'Baldy.'

'But he isn't.' His coat was thick, black and shiny as a seal's.

'He was when I got him.' A rescued animal. That was kind, but Mark's was not a gentle face. In the clarity of open air the lines showed from nose to mouth and scored across the forehead.

Kate had put him at around Alan's age. Alan was mid-thirties with hardly any lines on his face. She could smooth away Alan's frowns quickly and simply, but it would take more than light fingertip massage to rub out the furrow between Mark's dark straight brows. She wondered if anyone tried, and she smiled, partly at the dog jumping high and catching the stick in mid-air, but mostly at the idea of somebody saying, 'There, there,' to Mark, and gently stroking his brow.

When they finally arrived at her car, where her typewriter lay on the back seat under a travelling rug, she remembered food and that she must buy some. 'Where can I shop?' she asked, and he took her down an almost deserted street to a little self-service store.

The people they did pass looked more like locals than late holidaymakers. They got good mornings from most of them, and Kate was conscious of their inquisitive eyes on her.

They were the only customers in the shop. A cheerful-faced woman greeted them and watched them at the shelves, and when Kate put down her wire basket at the checkout the woman smiled broadly at her and at Mark standing beside her. He said, 'This is Miss Kershaw, she's staying at the tower.'

'*Very* nice,' said the woman, fairly twinkling as if Kate might have been a girlfriend rather than an out-of-season tourist, and Kate could hardly insist that she was a paying guest. 'Staying long, are you?' the woman probed.

'Two weeks,' said Kate. As the tower was for sale she might wonder if Kate was buying it; and Mark might also believe that Kate was a possible purchaser. Outside the shop she confessed, 'I'm glad I walked in on you yesterday, but really I was a trespasser. I couldn't buy the tower no matter how much I wanted to. Sorry I wasted your time.'

'I wouldn't say that,' he said.

Neither would Kate. None of their time together had been wasted time. It had been fun, with a little excitement, a little *frisson* of fear. But never dull. Now she asked, 'Are you going back?'

'I'm going to the shop.'

'May I come? I'd like to see your photographs.'

That seemed to amuse him, for the wide mouth quirked. 'Would you, now?' he said.

The shop with 'T. Brandon, Photographer,' on the weathered signboard was in a row of three-storey buildings. The upper windows were curtained, the two shop windows displaying mainly wedding photographs and some attractive child studies.

Kate stayed outside long enough to glance over them, and it was good professional work, although it was hard to imagine Mark getting the wedding groups together, holding up the toy to catch the baby's eye. She sensed an impatience in him, a quicksilver restlessness.

He was opening envelopes at a desk at the back of the shop, and she walked around, looking at some shots of gardens, students in graduation gowns, portraits. She stopped in front of the head-and-shoulders study of a girl, blonde hair tumbling loose, with such a glow of sexual eagerness about her that the luscious parted lips seemed to be whispering, 'Take me . . .'

Mark saw where she was looking and she said drily, 'As the lady said, *very* nice. Is she local?'

'Yes. She wanted it for a beauty competition a magazine was running.'

'Did she win?'

'She did.'

'I'm not surprised. Is she a model now?'

He said solemnly, 'Unfortunately she turned out to be only occasionally photogenic,' and she laughed,

'So this was a one-off? What did you do to get that sexy look?'

'Trick of the trade.' He leered at her. 'Take your picture?'

'I'd have to think about it.' Nothing he said would send her hot-eyed and panting, but a photograph might be a souvenir to take back to Alan. She changed the subject and asked, 'Is it mostly summer trade?'

'There's not much doing now.' He left mail and envelopes on the desk and came towards her. 'As it happens, I'm taking a break from work myself. I've got this hobby, photographing old buildings, churches, bits of statuary. So long as they've been around over two hundred years.'

'You're interested in the old days?'

'You could say that.'

'More than in what's happening now?' she asked.

She had bought a newspaper in the shop. It stuck out of her carrier bag of groceries. He opened it and glanced at page one, which as usual made gloomy reading. 'I take the present as it comes,' he said, 'when I have to.'

Of course he had to. Everybody had to. The present was where you lived, although you might escape for a little while. 'I suppose I should be carting this lot back,' Kate said.

'Leave it here for now. Come with me.'

'Where?'

He shrugged, and she knew it was not the tower that had given her that buzz of excitement, it was the man. Being near him was bringing that sixth sense into play, warning her that if she did not tag along she could be missing something sensational.

She might be safer missing it. He might take her where she did not want to go. But she said, 'Yes, all right,' and he put the frozen food packs into a small fridge in a little side room, and left the carrier bag with the rest on a table.

She took her newspaper with her and they went through a back door to a row of garages behind the buildings. His car was a large three-year-old BMW, but before Kate could climb in Baldy had shouldered her aside and settled down himself, completely filling the passenger seat.

'He knows I'm a trespasser,' she said, and when Mark ordered,

'In the back!' the dog dragged himself over like a geriatric convalescent and lay there glowering at her.

'Does he bear grudges?' she asked. 'If there's a risk that he might corner me some time and settle accounts he can keep his seat.'

'You're hurting his feelings—he wouldn't hurt a fly.'

'Hmm,' she said doubtfully, but with a rumble of resignation Baldy curled up and went to sleep.

The roads were almost empty, the car went smoothly and the man was a skilful driver. It was a new experience for Kate to be on the move and not know where she was going. So was taking a holiday alone where no one could find her. She felt so free and light-hearted that she found herself laughing softly.

Mark didn't ask why, but he smiled at her, a flash of white teeth against the tan of his skin, and she said, 'It was raining the last time I was here too, but you must have had your share of good weather.'

'We get our share of most things.' This morning he was wearing a check shirt under a brown leather jacket, and no pallor showed under his collar. After a hot summer the autumn rainfall had filled rivers and reservoirs again, and most summer tans were fading. Kate's had long gone. She was quite pale.

She pulled down the mirrored flap and grimaced at her washed-out reflection. She was combing her hair when they passed the caravans and cars parked on a wide grass verge. In spite of the rain doors were open. Dogs and children were running around, men and women were about.

Mark hooted and slowed down. He was recognised, because they all seemed to wave, and Kate wondered if this was where he was heading. But he wound down the window and called, 'Everything all right?' and getting an affirmative chorus wound the window up again and drove on.

'Friends of yours?' she asked. They had looked and sounded like friends.

'Yes.'

'Relations?'

No family, he had told her, but he could pass for a gypsy. 'I shouldn't think so,' he said. 'Thaddeus senior was not much of a traveller.'

'How about your mother?'

'Another homebody—so they tell me. I don't remember her, she died young.'

'I'm sorry,' said Kate.

He shrugged, dismissively, as though it hardly concerned him, and she supposed you couldn't grieve for someone you couldn't remember. She said wryly, and impulsively, 'My mother was a saint.'

'That must have been a trial for you,' and she heard herself telling him,

'It was, she really enjoyed being a martyr. When my father walked out everybody rallied around her and her poor fatherless child.'

'How old were you?' he asked.

'Thirteen.'

He still watched the road, which was empty but winding. 'Even then,' he said, 'you must have had the jaw that showed you were going to be nobody's victim.'

She didn't know she had a determined jaw. She knew she had high cheekbones, a straight nose and good teeth, and her chin seemed the right shape for the rest of her face. When she was a child they had said she looked sulky, but pity, like charity, could be depressing.

Her mother had wallowed in it. She had played the injured party for years. Until a lorry went out of control in the high street and she was standing in its path.

When Kate was here before, her parents were keeping up the appearance of being together, although it was no longer any kind of marriage. Bitter memories came flooding back, and she murmured, 'How time flies!'

Then when Mark looked questioningly at her she forced a smile, because the last thing anyone else wanted to hear about would be her childhood troubles. She watched the splattering rain on the windscreen, and said brightly, 'Where *has* the summer gone?' She held up the folded newspaper. 'It's the very last day of October, November starts tomorrow, and it seems hardly any time at all since the first crocuses were coming up.'

He leaned slightly across her newspaper. 'That settles where we're going,' he said.

'What does?'

'Not more than a ten-minute run. Be patient.'

A mystery tour could be fun. 'I hope it's under-cover,' she said, and he grinned.

'You can have my coat.'

'Thank you. You seem to be waterproof, so maybe I will.'

'Waterproof?' he queried.

'Look at my hair.' Her fine silky bob was wet and lank; all the combing had done was flatten it further. 'And look at yours.' His thick springy hair seemed to have shaken off the rain like a dog's coat.

'Rain obviously bounces off you,' she said. 'You've got to be waterproofed,' and she reached to touch.

Of course his hair was wet. Her fingers slid in and out and her breath caught. Then she said gaily, 'Well, part-proofed. Where are we going?'

'Wait and see.'

She did that. She leaned back in her seat, her arms folded, her hands tucked tightly away because her fingers were tingling.

When they stopped there was nothing much to be seen, except the signpost at the crossroads. Hedgerows edged the roads, and beyond the hedgerows were fields. A farmhouse and a cluster of buildings were far enough away to be on the skyline, and Kate asked, 'Is this it?'

As he was opening her door it obviously was. It seemed to suit Baldy, who was already out of the car, tail swishing and ready to go anywhere.

She looked up at the signpost. 'Or are we lost?'

'Through here.' The iron gate was narrow, hawthorns and brambles almost snagged them as they edged through. There was no track across the field, but the turf under the hedge seemed trampled, and Kate's jaw sagged.

'It isn't, is it?' she gasped.

The grass-covered mound had to be a grave. There was a glass jar containing plastic pink roses on it, shells and coloured stones, and a vase of fresh chrysanthemums on which raindrops glistened like dew.

'Here lies Hetty,' said Mark. 'More or less.'

'What does that mean?'

'That's she's a survivor.'

'*Is*?' she queried.

'Hetty the Bastard, proof of the saying ''You can't keep a good girl down.'' Found as a newborn baby in a ditch around 1750, and no trouble to anybody until she was fourteen, when the girl a young farmer was planning to marry was poisoned. Hetty had had her own plans for him, and it did look as if she had tipped his bride-to-be the hemlock.

'Anyhow, the verdict was guilty, and Hetty was given a lethal dose of the same and buried in unconsecrated ground outside the churchyard. A few weeks later she was up and about, still wearing her burial shift.'

Kate's eyes widened and he went cheerfully on, 'The locals thought she'd been living with the Devil while she was underground and kept clear of her, but when she died again, apparently from natural causes, they buried her again. This time under a huge rock that needed a team of horses to drag it into place.

'Being underground got her back on her feet. Before long she was back in circulation, and this time they got her for sheep-stealing and hanged her.

'She joined the congregation for Evensong that night, which must have cleared the church in record time. I always wondered what they were singing when Hetty sauntered in. After that there were five years while she lived in the woods, then in the best witch traditions the hunt followed a wounded hare that turned into Hetty.

'Now the charge was witchcraft, and she was sentenced to be burnt at the stake, then buried at the crossroads.'

Kate pointed to the ground and croaked, 'She's still there?'

'She made a bargain before they lit up. So long as the grave was well maintained she might stay buried, and as you can see, it is. No one admits to bringing them, but there are always flowers and ornamental touches. Especially today.'

She was catching on. 'Hallowe'en?'

'That's right. It was on Hallowe'en that she came back, and they do say she's been seen around since.'

'So she doesn't keep her promise?'

'Maybe sometimes she gets bored with the Devil.'

He probably has your colouring, she thought. Tall and thin and hungry-looking. She said, 'That's just the story for today. I'd hate to have missed that. Now can we get away from here?'

'We should be leaving something,' Mark told her.

'Like what? I'm not leaving anything with my fingerprints on. I don't want her tracking me down.'

He laughed and broke off a hedge sprig that still had a few wrinkled scarlet berries and offered it to her. She took it gingerly, avoiding the prickles, placed it between the shells and asked, 'What happened to the farmer who started it all, the one she wanted to marry when she was fourteen?'

'A good question,' he said approvingly. 'You're probably a good reporter.' He held the iron gate open, and although all this was banter she was as pleased with the compliment as if his opinion really mattered to her.

'There's no record of him,' he said. 'But if he had any sense he emigrated as soon as he heard Hetty was up for the first time.'

This time Baldy took the back seat with less fuss, and they drove along the coastline. Villages were so quiet they seemed empty. In the small towns there was plenty of parking space as pedestrians hurried along with hunched shoulders and bowed heads.

It rained without a break in the clouds, but the scenery made the ride worthwhile: the sea was almost always in sight. Kate would have settled for a round trip taking her back to the tower, but as they reached a black and white inn offering 'Good Food' Mark said, 'Shall we try here?' and it was lunchtime.

He went a few paces ahead of her across the foyer, and when the girl at the reception desk saw him coming, her face lit up in a wide bright smile, with what Kate took for delighted recognition. Although when Mark reached her he only said, 'May we have a table for two?'

She said of course, and led them into a small panelled dining-room and seated them by a window. She had hardly taken her eyes off Mark, Kate could have been invisible, and Kate could have sworn she was breathing fast. As she backed away Kate asked, 'Do you know each other?'

'No.' He was reading the menu. 'Why?'

Because she looked so pleased to see you. Because there are empty tables but trade doesn't seem that bad . . . But it was no concern of Kate's. 'Just wondering,' she said.

The food was traditional, which meant you knew more or less what you were getting and there was no need to discuss it. Kate had fish and Mark had steak and kidney pie. Another girl took their order, from Mark, even when Kate was reading out her own choice, and Kate studied her thoughtfully.

She had the same glow as her colleague in the foyer. And the beauty queen in the photograph. These two were not so blatant, but both of them

obviously fancied him rotten, and Kate held down
a fit of giggles.

She was used to women being smitten with Alan,
but she had never seen any female carrying on like
this at first sight of him. She had no doubt it was
first sight. They didn't know Mark Brandon, but
his male aura or charisma, or whatever you called
it, seemed to send them weak at the knees, and that
was quite funny when you were immune yourself.

Well, almost immune. Kate could have found him
physically attractive, but she wore Alan's invisible
ring, so no flirtation with another man was ever
going beyond words.

While Mark collected her groceries from the shop
Kate walked through the archway that led into the
street, looked at the photographs in the window
again and waited for him.

There were lights in the upper storeys. 'Do you
live here?' she asked as he came out of the shop.

'I've got a room. Come on.' He took her arm,
hurrying her away. He wasn't inviting her up there,
but he knew the tide times, and she strode along
beside him.

She collected her little typewriter from the car
and they ran with the dog through the rain, over
the wet stones of the causeway. She was in smooth-
soled shoes and, alone, she would have been scared
of slipping. But Mark was sure-footed from long
practice. She took his free hand and they went so
fast, reaching the rocks and climbing the steps, that
she was gasping for breath as he unlocked the door.

The shadowy room seemed as echoing and empty
as an underground cavern, and she hesitated, just
outside, until a light came on. Then she stepped in

and put her typewriter on the table. 'Is there enough hot water for a bath?' she asked.

There was, and it was bliss, getting out of her wet clothes and slipping into the warm scented water. She was tempted to stay submerged, because the bathroom was chilly and spartan—white-tiled walls and white suite, not even a rug on the linoed floor.

She put down a towel underfoot, and she had brought a bath gel with her that gave an illusion of luxury, filling the air with the fragrance of herbs and flowers.

She washed her hair under the shower, and the warmth on her skin lasted long enough for her to dress and put on a little make-up. But she went down with her hair still damp, and she was kneeling in front of the stove and running her fingers through her hair when Mark walked in.

'Praying?' he said.

'Praying it won't blow back on me while I'm drying my hair. What do you fancy for dinner?'

They started with soup again, and Kate knocked up a spaghetti bolognese. They were forking that down when she said, 'How quiet it is.'

'Does that bother you? Would you like some music?'

'No, but last night there was thunder rumbling all the time. And then the storm. That should have been tonight. Hallowe'en should have had the storm.'

It was peaceful in here, and again the man and the dog were good company. The lamp on the table threw a glow around them, softening Mark's face and, relaxed, his long body had an easy animal grace.

A second lamp burned in the window, and Kate joked, 'Should we have put a lamp in the window tonight?'

'You think Hetty might home in on it?'

She pulled a face. 'Let's move it.'

He got up and replaced the lamp on the table by a wall, and Kate went close to the windowpane, shielding her eyes, peering into the darkness. Clouds hid the stars, but in the pale moonlight she could see the lights of the town and make out the end of the causeway.

'What's that?' she squealed, because something white fluttered and danced where the causeway left the beach. A sheet of newspaper was being blown along. They both knew what it was although, crazily, it had startled her. 'If Hetty should come knocking,' she said, 'don't let her in.'

They were fooling, of course, and he said, 'An interview with Hetty would be quite a scoop for you.'

'I'm local radio. She wasn't one of *our* witches. You're the one with the hobby for photographing anything over two hundred years old. Can you take pictures of ghosts?'

'Oh, yes,' he said flatly, and that made her move away from the window to look at him. His face was masklike, but before she could speak he smiled. 'We're out of Hetty's range, I don't think we shall be seeing her tonight. They used to say it was the tinkers who tended her grave, but even when there are no travellers around the flowers still come.'

Back at the table he launched into travellers' tales, and Kate was fascinated. From boyhood he had been friendly with the families who camped, spasmodically, around here. He described them for her, ageing, changing; their traditions, their brushes with the law. She knew that modern times had to be tough for them, but listening to Mark was like reading a racy and hilarious book.

She did say, 'You should write a book,' and he said,

'Talking of books, what's yours about?'

Then she had to admit, 'It isn't my book. I'm just typing some of it and putting notes into order, for a friend.'

'The friend who lets you stroll off on your own?'

'The very one.' She was not confiding in Mark about Alan and she should be getting back to her own room. She yawned, covering her mouth with the back of her hand. 'Bedtime,' she said, and he reached across the table for her other hand.

'You won't be lying awake worrying about Hetty tonight? You wouldn't feel safer with company?'

She got her hand away quickly, he was holding it lightly. 'I'd feel a darn sight safer without company,' she said. 'I'll take my chances with Hetty.'

He was cheerfully unabashed. 'I thought you might,' and she said goodnight, laughing. Upstairs she smiled at Alan's photograph.

'No danger,' she said. 'No danger at all.'

Before she fell asleep she wondered what Mark had meant about photographing ghosts.

She woke early. It was hardly light and still raining, and she crept downstairs to bring up a chair she could sit on while she worked at the table by the window. The stairs were stone, so there was no creaking there, but Baldy began to bark just before she got back to her room. He was up here somewhere, but he shut up quite soon, and she took the stack of manuscript from her briefcase.

She had done some of the typing before and now she copied afresh, dealing with corrections and insertions, keys clattering, and her mind concentrating so that she literally jumped when Mark spoke.

He must have passed this way earlier. Now he was coming back from the bathroom, bare-legged and bare-chested, a knotted towel slung round his hips, asking her, 'This is his best side, is it?'

He had spotted Alan's photograph and was giving it a professional scan from the doorway, and Kate swung round in her chair.

As it happened, Alan did prefer his right profile to be photographed, but she said coolly, 'Not particularly. Unlike your beauty queen, he's photogenic from any angle.'

'If you say so.' He came into the room, and stood with his back to her, surveying the photograph over her unmade bed. His back was smooth and brown and tautly muscular. He said, 'A few years ago he'd have been holding a pipe.'

'He doesn't smoke.'

'I bet he doesn't.' What was funny about that? But she was sure he was smiling. 'Definitely a half-a-Mars-bar man,' he said.

'*What*?' she queried.

'Never trust a man who leaves half a Mars bar. He'll never go all the way on anything.'

'What a load of——'

'Another thing—while we were holding hands last night.'

'We were not——' Kate began.

'I noticed that your heart line snarls up your head line. You want to watch that.'

'That's the Romany in you, is it? I don't suppose you'd know a head line from a heart line if they rose up and hit you.' She leaned over the back of her chair and stretched an arm towards him, the palm of her hand upwards 'Go on, tell me which is which.'

Mark was holding the towel at his waist as if it might slip if he moved hastily, and when he said, 'I'm not dressed for palm reading,' she changed her mind, turned away, and put both her hands back on the keyboard.

If the towel dropped she didn't think it would embarrass him unduly, but she could blush to the roots of her hair. 'See you over breakfast,' he said. 'As you're up and about you might get the coffee on.'

She was not about. She was sitting here typing. But there was plenty of time to do all she had promised to do with the book. She was supposed to be self-catering and she wanted a cup of coffee, so she tidied her papers, made her bed, and went downstairs to the kitchen.

After last night she was at home here. A few minutes had been long enough to familiarise her with the layout and the equipment. It was basic: a stove, a sink, and a fridge, a working surface, pots and pans in cupboards, crockery in a variety of patterns on the shelves.

A small pantry was stocked mostly with tins, but there was a coffee percolator, so this morning they would have real coffee rather than instant, and she went around breathing in the aroma of roasted beans while she laid the table and watched that the toast didn't flare up under the grill.

Someone would probably make a luxury kitchen of this when the tower was sold, and she envied them. She had had a lot of pleasure fixing and furnishing her own little end-of-terrace house. When she put that up for sale she would be sad to see it go, but where they lived would depend on Alan's career.

When Mark came down with the dog Kate had just poured herself a cup of coffee and was looking through the window. It was a bleak morning out there, and she asked, 'What are you doing today?'

'Nothing in particular. Care to join us?'

'Yes,' she said.

They had breakfast, cleared up and set off, and that became their regular morning routine. Whoever came down first got breakfast and after breakfast they walked Baldy along the shore, then sometimes took Mark's car, sometimes Kate's, and hit the road.

As with all good holidays, the days passed quickly, and in spite of the appalling weather Kate was having a riotous time. It was like finding a boon companion on a foreign shore, who you would probably never meet again once you were home.

For now they were inseparable all day long, day after day. But she slept alone. Her situation had been clear from the start. The photograph by her bed was the man in her life. That was understood and accepted.

Women fancied Mark all right. She looked out for their reactions now, it was her own little joke, so maybe a woman who didn't made a change for him and something of a relief. He knew that he could flirt outrageously with Kate, because she would never take him seriously.

On the second Wednesday it was still raining. It must have stopped from time to time, but never long enough to do any good. Each night she washed her hair and every morning she got it wet again. Mostly they ignored the rain, the only sightseers doing the beauty spots, viewing ruins, walking beaches and under dripping trees along streams that were turning into torrents.

Kate wore a plastic mac over her coat, and indoors their shoes squelched. On Wednesday they squelched around the Barn, a row of farm outbuildings that had been turned into a mighty secondhand furniture and bric-à-brac mart.

There were several cars in the car park. It was a place for bargains at any time of the year, and inside masses of furniture, from three-piece suites to deepfreezes, were stacked high. Customers prowled along the narrow aisles. Sometimes excited cries rang out, 'Look at that dresser, it's pine under the paint! Can you get it out? How much is it?'

A young couple were unrolling a large rug, and as Kate and Mark passed them the girl smiled up at Kate, 'Good, isn't it?' They were shopping for their home, she presumed Kate and Mark were, and Kate thought wryly that Alan wouldn't be seen dead in a place like this. Dust in the air prickled her nose, and although the warehouses were heated she shivered.

Upstairs were smaller objects, on long trestle tables and shelves, the walls hung with pictures, amateur watercolours, faded prints. Kate was going to buy something for the fun of it, and if she took her time she might find something special, although this was biggish business, and hidden treasure was unlikely to have slipped by the dealer-owners

It was dusty up here too, she could hardly stop sneezing. She dabbed her nose with a tissue and picked up a lustre dish. That was good value, but a small elephant that looked like ebony but was plastic had an endearing air about him.

And there were some battered old toys. A doll's house was cumbersome and beyond her price range, but the puppets were comical. She slid the strings of one off its rod and it lurched drunkenly on the edge of the table.

'Muffin the Mule,' she said.

'That's no mule,' said Mark. 'It's got the wrong ears.'

'So he's Harry the Horse. I'll have him.'

He took the puppet from her and went to a patrolling assistant, and Kate started to sneeze again. She was not shivering now, she was warming up. Mostly in her head, which felt as if it was filling with warm cotton wool.

She had been slightly off-colour from breakfast—nothing worth mentioning, but in this stuffy atmosphere she was suddenly exhausted.

She sat down on a horsehair sofa, and when Mark came back, swinging Harry the Horse from a forefinger, she said, 'I think I got wet through once too often, I think I've caught a chill.'

He put a cool hand on her warm forehead and she sneezed on cue, and he said, 'Let's go.'

Her eyes were watering now, and she really should have expected this. Since she was here she had spent most of her days in the rain, and if that was not chilling the system, what was?

Once she was back in the tower a hot drink and some aspirins would soon sweat it out of her. In the meantime it helped to have Mark to lean on going down the stairs, because her knees were almost as wobbly as the puppet's.

The couple with the rug were putting it into the boot of their car. As Kate tottered out on Mark's arm they looked across the car park and the man called, 'Is your wife all right?'

'She will be as soon as I get her home,' said Mark, and the girl smiled knowingly, while Kate thought, it's this mac, she thinks I'm pregnant.

She had to smile at that herself, but she knew that if she had been alone, she would have walked out of the Barn and across the car park without staggering. She was not ill. She had the start of a cold in the head, which was no big deal. But it had been intoxicating to let somebody take care of her, to know that if she slumped she would be caught.

She could not remember anyone ever catching and carrying her. There had been no loving arms around her as a child. When she grew to be a woman embraces had been either casual or sexual. Of course, if she had been with Alan, feeling groggy, he would have been as solicitous as Mark, and in the car the dizziness had passed.

She dug into her handbag for another tissue and began to laugh. 'They've not only given you a wife, did you notice that she was giving you a family as well? It's all this padding I'm wearing.'

He grinned. 'And they think all we've bought for the poor little beggar is a knackered nag.'

The puppet's strings had tangled. When Mark held it up now the joints were crazily awry, and Kate gave a cry of mock anguish. 'That's got to be hurting! Come here, Harry, let's see what we can do about getting you back into shape.'

She untwined the knots as they drove along, and when the strings swung loose she hung the puppet on the mirror hinge and said, 'See? All that's needed are the healing hands.'

'You'll have to wait till we get back,' he said, and she gave a snort of laughter through her blocked-up nose.

'You keep your hands off me!'

'And there's this old gypsy recipe for ague.'

'Of course there is, but I'll stay with the aspirins.'

They were in Mark's car, and this afternoon he parked it beside hers on the waterfront. The tide was going out, the final stepping-stones of the causeway were hardly above water, and once inside the tower the chill from the walls seemed to be creeping into her bones.

Mark found a thermometer after a search, and her teeth chattered on it, although the mercury was higher than normal. Then he got the stove glowing and brought in a Calor gas radiator, and Kate kicked off shoes and peeled off tights and outer clothing, and lay wrapped in a duvet in a deep arm-chair, her feet up on a stool.

She had never pampered a head cold like this before. When Mark produced two steaming tumblers of amber liquid and told her, 'The gypsy cure,' she sipped and said,

'And it tastes just like whisky and lemon.'

'They're a cunning race. But to show there's no risk involved I'm sharing it with you.' He raised the other glass. 'Your very good health.'

'To health and happiness,' she said. She had had a happy holiday. Mark had been a marvellous companion, with never a sign of that black mood she had glimpsed that first night. Whatever his troubles were they were not for sharing.

And why should they be? None of their talk had been soul-searching. They were just a couple who liked each other and amused each other, and although she might leave him her address it would be no surprise if he disliked letter writing and never bothered to contact her.

She dozed on and off, feeling a fraud. This was pure laziness, but lying here was therapeutic. Mark and Baldy lounged around too, the dog sleeping, the man reading, and the whisky and lemon was as good a treatment as any secret recipe. The ache in her bones had gone and she thought her head was clearing.

When she opened her eyes and Mark was not in the room she listened for him, and when he came back she smiled. The picture was incomplete without him, like a piece missing from a jigsaw.

'I've put a hot water bottle in your bed,' he said. 'I don't think it leaks, I shook it around.'

'Thank you.' It was time for bed. She went to the bathroom, sponged down and got into a night-shirt. She was sure she had caught her chill in time. It might drag on for a few days, but it would develop into nothing worse than a few sniffles and sneezes.

He had said he would bring her another hot drink, and the bed was warm. She sat up, the duvet pulled up to her chin, until Mark stood by her bed, and then she took the mug from him. 'Same again,' she said. 'My cold may have gone by morning, but I could have a hangover.'

'Take the tablets.'

She swallowed them and knew that if he had sat down beside her and put his arms around her she would have drawn him hungrily against her. It might have been the whisky or the slight fever, but suddenly she was wanting him, with a craving as though she was starving.

He smiled and said goodnight and went, and Kate held the steaming mug very carefully because the rocky foundations of the tower seemed to be shaking.

She fixed her eyes on Alan's photograph and tried to feel thankful that she was safe. That could have been madness, making a mockery of love, and it had to be a warning that she was losing touch with reality.

All this, Mark most of all, was here today and gone tomorrow, like a dream or a film. Reality was Alan, and the people and places she would be returning to at the end of the week. She had sent a few cards home, saying how awful the weather was but that she was enjoying the break. But nobody knew her address and, apart from that, she had hardly given them a thought.

Of course she had thought about Alan. He was at the back of her mind always because she loved him. But she had not touched the typewriter again. She had done no work at all after a couple of hours that morning.

Tomorrow was Thursday, she was leaving on Saturday. For the last two days she would definitely get down to it because, what with one thing and another, her conscience was going into overdrive.

*　　*　　*

Next morning, apart from a rather pink nose and a tendency to sniff, her cold was no problem. But it was still raining, and even if the sun had been shining she had finished gadding about.

'Good idea,' said Mark, when she explained that today she would be working in her room.

He was first down, and she sat at the table drinking coffee. She didn't stay for breakfast. She was not hungry yet. When she was she could come down to the kitchen and take up something on a tray, disturbing her train of thought as little as possible. She wanted no interruptions today, and she did ask, 'Is there likely to be anyone wanting to view?'

'If there is the agent will show them round. Just ignore them.'

'I will.'

For a while she heard Baldy barking and knew they were walking along the beach. When that faded there were only the seabirds, and a haze of rain on the windowpane and all the isolation she needed.

Alan's book might not be ready for publication for a few years yet, not until his political career took off. It was a diary, a journal, jotting down his thoughts, describing places he visited, people he met. As a journalist Kate was helping him get it into shape, and some of it she felt was really inspiring.

Typing it was like listening to his voice, and when she looked at his photograph he seemed to be smiling at her, keeping her doggedly at her labour of love.

Her back stiffened just before her eyes started to smart. She had been poring over papers for hours, and when she sat back this time she knew that she was due for a break. More coffee maybe, or tea, and she should be getting herself something to eat.

She had had all her meals with Mark, and dinner tonight would be no different. There was food in the fridge and the cupboard. Until then she sliced cheese and spread crackers and ate them in the kitchen. The cheese was bland, although it was labelled, 'mature'. Her cold must be dulling her tastebuds. She made herself finish the first cracker and dropped the second in the wastebin.

Lovely peace and quiet. Nothing stopping her working. She wondered what Mark was doing and how long it would be before he came back. The tide was in. It would need a dinghy to reach the tower now, and this was a hell of a place to be marooned.

She had never felt this way before. Well, she had never been alone before. She remembered what he had said about photographing ghosts, but the tower shouldn't be haunted. No battles had been fought here, never a shot fired in anger. It was just that it seemed so vast and so empty without Mark. As though the tower missed him, as though she missed him.

The sooner she got back to her own little world the better. There was no reason why she couldn't go tomorrow, and in her room she lay on her bed planning to do that. She would rest awhile and then she would pack. Right now mild depression was draining her.

She woke hearing the dog bark, and reacted automatically, almost leaping into her chair by the table. She didn't want Mark to know that she had not spent an enthralling day with Alan's book. She didn't stop to wonder why it mattered, but she banged the keys briskly, and when he said, 'Hi!' she did a double-take, and lied,

'You startled me—I never heard you.'

'All right?' he asked.

'Just fine.'

'How's it going?'

'Very well. It's very good.'

He was standing by the table she was using as a desk, and she couldn't cover every page and fling herself over the typewriter. Shouting 'No!' would have been just as melodramatic.

When he said, 'May I?' he was already reading, and she snapped,

'You are, aren't you?'

'Is it a novel?'

'No.' It was rather like betraying Alan's confidence, although the book was hardly a secret. 'He's into politics,' she said coolly. 'And that page you've just picked up helps to explain some of the reasons why.'

To help others, because he cared.

It was one of Kate's favourite pieces. When Alan read it to her she had said it was almost a poem.

'Very touching,' said Mark, and she looked at him sharply as he picked up another page and asked, 'He goes on like this, does he?'

'Do you mind?' she said tartly, and he murmured,

'Not at all,' reading fast and looking more amused than impressed. 'Well, he's got the makings of a politician,' he said, 'high-falutin' and long-winded.' Kate whipped back the page and she could have hit him.

Instead she drawled, 'You're a small-town man with a small-town mind, but some men have wider visions,' and he laughed then.

'You should take this in smaller doses, you're talking like it,' and she had to bite her lip to keep quiet until he was out of the room.

He was insufferably rude, and she was seething. If she went downstairs she was going to start arguing with him. What had he done with his life, except inherit his father's shop and follow his father's trade? Because he had no ambition himself that gave him no right to sneer at Alan.

And she was stupid to give a damn what Mark thought about anything. She was leaving here tomorrow and she was in half a mind to go now.

But that would mean travelling in darkness before the end of her journey. She didn't mind night driving, but she was jaded, and it would make more sense to wait till morning. Then she could call up friends from home and spend tomorrow evening in congenial company. And on Saturday she could drive to the airport to meet Alan's flight.

Suddenly she was missing them all. Not only Alan, but her workmates and her girlfriends. She needed to get in touch with them again, to tell them she had stayed in a Martello tower and it had never stopped raining. To make a joke of being taken to Hetty's grave on Hallowe'en as the high spot of her holiday, and buying a tatty puppet as her spending spree.

'I won't be sorry to get back,' she would say, 'and what's your news?' There were plenty of numbers she could ring to put her in a mood cheerful enough to get through a final meal with Mark without losing her temper.

She would tell him she was leaving in the morning, and settle up, and if he should ask for her address she would say her own house was on the market so she didn't have a permanent address herself, because she did not want him contacting her again.

She didn't see him on her way out, so there was no need to explain where she was going, there was no phone in the tower. She didn't look back, and when she reached the sea-front she went to the box outside the little post office just up the road. The sea breeze was chilly and she was glad to find the box empty and the phone working.

She rang a friend who lived in the same street, who had been keeping an eye on her house while she was away, and got no reply.

Next she tried Jenny, who worked with her and would surely have some office gossip after nearly two weeks. 'Hello,' said Kate after Jenny answered. 'It's me, Kate. How are things?'

She heard Jenny's shuddering sigh before she wailed, 'Oh, Kate—oh, it's *awful*! Oh, I am so *sorry* for you!'

CHAPTER THREE

It HAD to be Alan. There had to have been an accident. Kate's blood ran cold and she gripped the phone as if it was her support. 'Kate?' Jenny quavered after a few moments. 'Are you there?'

'What's happened?'

'You don't know? Where are you?'

What did it matter if she was on the moon? Kate said through stiffening lips, 'You're the first person from home I've spoken to since I came away. What has happened?'

'Oh, no...' Jenny didn't want to be the one to break the news. 'We've been trying to find you. Your friends.' She gulped and Kate thought, I shall go mad, for heaven's sake tell me! She couldn't speak herself.

'It's Alan,' said Jenny. 'He came back. Celia Chambers was with him.'

No accident. Nobody was hurt. Kate waited, and Jenny went stumbling on, 'She was with him while he was away. Since they got back they've been together all the time. You know who her father is.'

An ex-member of the Cabinet who still had powerful political clout. Sure Kate knew, and that Alan would be delighted to get Clifford Chambers on his side. Daughter Celia was a pretty girl who was in the local news from time to time, and Alan could have been making up to her. They could have met while he was on his business trip and something brought him back early, and since then a meal together would be enough to start the gossip.

Jenny should have been an agony aunt instead of a secretary, she could be relied on to make a crisis out of next to nothing. 'Just as well I'm coming back tomorrow,' Kate said lightly, and Jenny said,

'It's been going on for months—Celia's been talking. They wanted her father's OK, so it's all been hush-hush, it's been an affair for ages.'

Kate felt as though she had stepped on a step that wasn't there, a lurching of the stomach and a rising nausea. 'I think it's wicked!' Jenny sounded close to tears. 'The way he used you. We're all so angry for you, it's been a rotten trick, because you had no idea, had you?'

Kate could almost see a tear rolling down Jenny's pink cheek, her big brown eyes more like a mournful spaniel than ever, and she said, 'As the man said, "Things are rarely what they seem".'

Then she hung up and somebody was waiting outside. As Kate walked out of the phone box the woman who was shivering in the wind said, 'Isn't it bitter?'

Kate nodded. She could taste the bitterness, but she hardly felt the ice-edged wind. She must speak to Alan. It was always possible that Jenny was recounting hearsay rather than fact. If Alan was home she could ring his home and get through to him some way.

They might laugh together about this, although he should be angry, because it was—well, it was bitter. It was horrible. She must talk to him, but she couldn't do that right away.

She went back to the sea-front and got into her car and wondered if she should just drive home. Without her luggage, without paying for her lodgings. That would give her long lonely hours on the road, but in the end she would have to pick up a phone and dial the number she knew so well and ask for Alan.

She was scared sick. She believed in him and she trusted him, but she remembered how it was when she was nineteen and two days before what should have been their wedding day Philip phoned to say that he was sorry, so sorry, but his mother was right, they were too young.

Mother had been right. They would have grown irrevocably apart, and Kate had had such sympathy from her friends who had all pitied her and told her she was not to blame, it was not her fault. Poor Kate!

But if it was happening again that would mean there had to be a flaw in her, something radically wrong. If Alan answered the phone and said, 'I'm so sorry——' she thought she would die.

She drove into the nearest town and stopped at the first hotel that was open to non-residents. She could phone from here in warmth and comfort, but not just yet. She couldn't sit around in the lounge bar because she must not drink and drive, but she had to pass the time somehow, so she had dinner.

She must be hungry, she had only eaten a cracker and cheese today and not all that much yesterday. Hollowness was a kind of hunger, and she selected with care: soup, fish, sorbet ice to finish. Food that should slide past the constriction in her throat.

She ate slowly, and afterwards she could not have described one fellow diner, nor even what the room looked like. What loomed ahead of her filled her mind so that nothing else was getting through.

The condemned woman ate a hearty meal, she thought; and when she could put it off no longer, she paid her bill and went into a phone booth off the foyer and dialled.

She got Alan's mother, a sweet vague woman who yelped, 'Kate!' sounding as if she had jumped like a frightened rabbit. 'I'll get Alan,' she said, and Kate heard the phone clatter from her fingers.

Then Alan's voice saying, 'Kate?'

He knew she was there. All she had to do was stand with the phone to her ear, she didn't have to say a word. 'God, Kate, I'm so sorry,' he said. She put down the phone and she didn't die, because she had known what he was going to say.

The blow to her heart had come when she talked to Jenny. Now there was only numbness inside her. Where her heart used to be was emptiness. Which showed that the heart was not essential to a living body, you could manage without one. She was not going to die, but she could be going crazy. And it would get worse, when she had to go back and face them all.

She drove along the coastline with the deliberation of a learner driver—heaven knew why. She wouldn't much care if she went over a cliff, but all her movements were slowed down as if a mainspring had broken.

She parked in the same spot, overlooking the bay and the water. For almost the first time both the moon and the stars were out. When she turned out the car headlights the causeway was a bright silver path in the dark silver sea.

It was a night for memories. Her second jilting bringing back the first, as another man chose not to spend his life with her. She should have remembered that marriage brought no happiness. Her parents' marriage should have warned her not to get that involved with anyone.

When she was last here as a child she had crept away from a scene between them, and looked at the tower and wished she could hide in it. She remembered loneliness well. The tower had seemed like a haven then, and now she had nowhere else to go.

There were lights on in the windows, and when she stepped on to the third great flat stepping-stone she saw the door open and light streamed out on to the rock. Mark was silhouetted at the top of the steps; he must have seen her car, and she hurried and felt cold water lapping over her feet.

The tide was coming or going. She was two-thirds of the way, and it had to be getting deeper because the path was disappearing under the waves. She was not turning back. She would wade. She knew there were currents, but she also knew the pattern of the causeway, and in her present near-zombie state pressing on was almost automatic; even when the waves reached her waist and she could feel them dragging the heavy skirt of her coat.

If they reached her chin she could swim, she was a strong swimmer and it was no distance. Then suddenly the current swirled around her, plucking her off the stones and sucking her down with the waters closing over her head.

She came up choking and spluttering, shoes and clothes weighing like lead, struggling to keep afloat. She was not panicking yet, but it was taking all her strength, and Mark surfacing beside her was welcome as a lifeline.

She probably would have reached the rocks herself, but she let him take the strain, hanging on to him while he supported her over the strip of water and hauled her up on to the rocks.

Out of the water her sodden clothing bogged her down, sprawling and choking, and he grabbed her again, raising her so that she managed to stumble along.

He said nothing until they were up the stone steps and into the tower, then he released her with a shove that nearly had her off her feet again. 'You stupid woman,' he roared. 'Didn't you hear me? They must have heard me in the bloody town!'

Shouting, 'Go back!' she supposed, and no, she had not heard, and if she had she would have taken no notice. Water was streaming from her, she was standing in a pool of sea-water, and his jeans and shirt were sticking to him.

'Get into some dry clothes,' he said wearily, as if she was an idiot who hadn't realised she was wet.

She unbuttoned her coat and left it on the flagstones, she doubted if she could have dragged herself upstairs in that. She left her shoes too and went straight to the bathroom. Thank goodness for hot water. She mustn't use it all, but her skin was blue with cold and she crouched over the warm rising steam.

She could have drowned just now and all her problems would have been over, but instead she'd been fighting like mad to get ashore. She would have made it, she thought, but she was grateful to Mark. Life might be hell, but she must have wanted to go on living.

The water rose in the bath and she slid in, lying low so that it covered as much of her freezing flesh as possible. She was so cold that the warm water almost scalded her, and then the returning blood circulation brought an agonising rush of pins and needles.

Physically the shock treatment was helping to clear her mind, although what Alan had done still seemed unbelievable.

It would be wonderful not to believe it. She had given him no time to explain. She had hung up as soon as he said, 'I'm so sorry.' He could have been going on to say, 'About these rumours that are going round.'

But not in that voice, with that groan of guilt. Nor would his mother have squealed and dropped the phone. As Jenny said, Kate had not had a clue. Or had she? Maybe later she would look back, spotting the clues that she had missed.

She hadn't had a clue with Philip either. Except for the big one, the way his mother kept harping about them being so young. And afterwards it had taken years before Kate had any real confidence in herself again.

This was worse. This left her with no pride at all. She had been conned and discarded and she remembered the promise she had made to herself, when she had believed she had a good life and that Alan loved her: Nobody is ever going to feel sorry for me again.

The rap on the door made her reach for a towel; she had been sitting naked on the side of the bath. 'Are you all right in there?' Mark called.

'Yes, I'll be right out.'

She let out the water and took a bigger towel and ran along to her room. She dressed quickly, in a skirt and her thickest jumper. Her only coat wouldn't be dry for ages and then it would probably be ruined, and it was a little miracle that when it dragged her under the water it hadn't kept her down.

She must thank Mark. He had just taken an icy swim because of her, and if she couldn't give him much of an explanation he was surely owed an apology.

He didn't seem any the worse. He was dry and changed, barefooted, and his hair was tousled. He was glaring at her as he demanded, 'Were you drunk?'

'*No!*' She had swallowed rather too much sea-water, but she didn't feel like joking, and he hardly looked in a humorous mood.

'Then why did——'

'I didn't hear you.'

'You must have gone stone deaf! And didn't it occur to you when you got up to your waist in it that you should have turned back?'

Her eyes held no light, they were wide and dark. 'I had to get here,' she said. He didn't ask why, but he looked steadily at her until she spoke again. 'I've just phoned Alan.'

'And?'

'This break was to give us both space to stand back and think,' although it had been nothing of the sort for her.

'And?' Mark repeated, and she managed a small shrug and a wry smile.

'We seemed to have moved further apart.' She added quickly, 'But don't say you're sorry.'

'Should I?'

'I don't think so. I don't think it's such a bad thing.' She was surprising herself, sounding so calm and reasonable when she was in such a turmoil, and she wondered if she could fool Jenny and the rest so that nobody would know how hurt she was.

'How about another slug of the gypsies' cure-all? That dip can't have done you much good.'

'You are kind,' she muttered.

'No,' he contradicted her flatly. 'But you're a crazy lady and I don't want you leaving here with pneumonia.'

'I wish——' she started. Then she bit her lip while he poured the drinks. She was wishing she need never leave to go back to what was waiting for her. Celia Chambers was rich and gorgeous, apart from her father's political pull. Kate's friends might think that Alan had behaved badly, but not many people would blame him for choosing Celia.

What competition was Kate? Poor Kate, coming back from her holiday alone to hear that Alan had been spending his days and nights with Celia.

She reached for the glass Mark was offering and gulped a little and coughed. She was still deeply shocked, or the pain would have been sharper instead of this dull ache.

When she got back she was going to be so alone, but this had not been a lonely holiday. She had spent it with a man sexy enough to have women drooling wherever he went. He was stunningly attractive. Nobody would feel sorry for Kate if they saw who she had spent her days with, and most of them would soon start wondering about the nights.

She wished they could meet him, they wouldn't pity her then, and inspiration burst on her so that she almost sat up beaming. She stopped herself in time. She must make it just a suggestion, because they got on so well together and her home was open house to her friends.

'You should be photographing some of the old places around where I live,' she said casually.

'Should I?'

'Here's an idea, how about a deal? I owe you for my lodgings; why don't you come back with me and have a holiday in *my* tower? Actually it's a terraced house overlooking the canal, but there's a spare room and all mod cons. Dogs welcome.'

She sipped her drink until he said, 'Sounds promising,' and triumph rose in her. She was promising nothing. No man was getting that kind of power over her again, but Mark could be her shield and her revenge.

She smiled and asked, 'Will you come?' and he said,

'Yes.'

Her chattering voice sounded jerky in her ears as she listed some of her local places of interest, promising to take him along, and asked, 'Are you just snapping away for fun? Any plans for what you might do with them?'

'Freelance sales. Perhaps a book eventually.' Then with a sardonic lift of an eyebrow, 'But don't worry, I won't ask you to do the typing.'

If that was a dig she had to ignore it, and she stretched across to stroke the dog. Baldy's thick shiny pelt was so damp that her fingers came away wet. 'He never went in too!' she gasped.

She hadn't noticed, but she had had no time or strength for looking around her. Grabbing Mark and getting ashore had been all that she could manage.

Mark smiled, 'He's not a dog who thinks before he jumps.'

So the dog had followed his master blindly into the dark sea. Kate said, 'I didn't do much thinking myself. I was a dope getting swept off the causeway, but I am a strong swimmer.'

'For all I knew you might not have been able to swim a stroke.' He didn't know much about her, nor she about him, but he could have saved her from drowning, and she said,

'Well, thank you, both of you. I can swim, but I wasn't dressed for it, and your help was much appreciated. Sorry you both had to get wet.'

'Not many times when we've been dry these past two weeks,' he joked. 'Total immersion seems a fitting finale,' and she giggled.

'Where do we go from here? Whatever next?'

'Warmer water?' Somehow Mark made that sound highly suggestive, and she thought, whatever you have in mind, from swimming in a foreign sea to sharing a bath, could turn into very hot water indeed. She laughed and said,

'Speaking for myself, I'm keeping dry for a while,' and it was odd that she could laugh when she was crying inside. She put down her glass and stood up. 'I left my coat and shoes downstairs, I wouldn't give much for their chances.'

They were where she had left them, the coat a sodden black heap, the shoe leather dulled and saturated. She poked the coat with the toe of the shoe she was wearing now. It was a dead water-logged weight, and only last month it had been her pride and joy—a classic trenchcoat in cashmere and pure new wool, costing more than she had ever paid for a coat before.

Now it was sea-wrack, rubbish, but nothing compared with everything else she had lost today. She managed to drag it over the back of one of the wooden chairs, and it felt as slimy as a sea creature. She could have been as clammy cold herself if Mark had not been looking out for her. She was not glad to be alive, she didn't think she ever would be again, but she turned away quickly from the grotesque shapelessness of the black coat and almost ran up the stairs.

From the doorway she told him, 'I'm having an early night, it's been a busy day and I still have my packing to do. Could we leave early in the morning?'

'Sure.'

'Do you have to tell anyone? Make any arrangements?'

'I'll be ready when you are,' he said.

Kate packed methodically, not thinking about anything that was outside this room. She could block out. It was a knack she had learned when she was very young. She could not have made it a way of life, she could only manage it for brief periods, but while she filled her case and got her bits and pieces together she held back the pain that could have overwhelmed her.

Her hands shook slightly as she put the manuscript into her briefcase, but she snapped down the fasteners and toyed with the idea of going out on to the rocks and chucking the lot into the sea. It was an appealing thought, except that Mark and Baldy might catch her at it and Mark might say,

'If you're that overwrought over Alan how will you be when you get back home? What kind of a set-up am I walking into?'

She didn't look at the photograph. She picked it up from the bedside table, carried it to the case and dropped it in face down. Then she covered it with a plastic bag in which her wet clothes were wrapped in her bathrobe, and soon afterwards she closed the case. She wouldn't think about unpacking tomorrow, but as she undressed she wondered fleetingly if tomorrow might make everything right again.

Maybe Alan would be waiting with an explanation that she could believe, and then she would have to explain why Mark was with her. He was a friend, and friends often stayed in her home, and of course it was platonic.

In bed the sheets were cold and in the darkness she knew that Alan would never again draw her into his arms and tell her he loved her. It was over, and, although Mark must never guess, she was clinging to him as desperately as she had when the waters were closing over her.

She didn't expect to sleep, but she did, although her rest was broken by dreams that just missed the jagged edge of nightmares. She couldn't remember her dreams when she woke, but sleeping and waking were much the same, grey and cold.

She washed and dressed and put colour on her face, then stood in the middle of her room like an actress in the wings psyching herself up for a performance.

Mark was in the kitchen, and she had to pretend that this morning was like all the others, except that it was the end of her holiday here. She must be bright and cheerful or he could turn those piercing eyes on her and see inside her head where her mind was running wild.

She might not be able to look straight at him for a while, but her voice came out all right. 'Wouldn't you know the rain had stopped?' She must have noticed that, although she didn't know when.

'Ain't it the way?' he said, and she stood back surveying her coat over the chair. It was drying stiff as a board and her shoes were rimed with salt. None of this would ever be wearable again.

'You'd have thought the shoes would have slipped off, wouldn't you?' she babbled. 'Do you mind if I leave them? How do you deal with your junk?'

'Leave it,' he said.

'If the estate agent brings anybody round the coat could give them a nasty shock.' She walked round it. 'In a dim light it could look like something very sinister sitting at your table. And what with that and the incredibly belching stove...'

He laughed, and she had to steady down or she could tip over into hysteria. She drank coffee and made herself eat some toast, and discuss rationally where they could stop for a break on the way. If the two cars got parted they decided to make for the car park of the Royal Oak, a hotel in a market town on the route.

They carried cases over the causeway. Mark had a holdall, and Kate said, 'You travel light,' but of course he would only be staying a few days, and when they reached their cars she looked back at the tower, bidding it a silent farewell, and asked, 'Have you had any offers yet?'

'Nothing final.'

'Well, if I come into money in the next few weeks I'll make you an offer myself.'

He knew she was joking. 'Got expectations, have you?'

'Oh, great expectations,' she said gaily. All she was expecting was anguish and heartache, but she was practising flippancy.

His car followed hers at first. Travelling alone she could have been weeping. Her head cold still caused the occasional sniffle, but real grief could have engulfed her, although she was not given to tears. Sometimes stories she was covering, tragedy, heroism, misted her eyes, but it was years since she had wept for herself.

She could have been weeping now, but when she saw Mark's car in the driving mirror she managed a ghost of a smile, although of course he couldn't see her expression. She was trying to block Alan out of her mind, so she turned on the radio and began to catch up on what was happening to the rest of the world.

It really had been a crazy fortnight. After the first day or two she had stopped buying newspapers. There was no TV in the tower and they hadn't listened to the radio news. From the sound of things they hadn't missed much, nothing had changed for the better.

Kate's personal life had changed terribly for the worse, but she wouldn't think about that now. When they got out of their cars and were together again she would say, 'I see what you meant about only taking the present when you have to. I've been listening to the news, and if somebody would stop the world I'd like to get off.'

She lost him driving through a busy town and swore fervidly as though it was a real loss, although he knew where they were meeting, he would be making his way there, and when she turned into the hotel car park she saw that he had arrived ahead of her.

She waved, passing his car, and parked near and sat at the wheel, undoing her seat-belt, collecting her handbag, and it was oddly comforting to watch the tall man with his long loose stride and the great black dog coming towards her.

As she climbed out Baldy swished a tail and Mark held out a hand that she took. Of course, she could have got out of the car without stumbling, but it was good to touch him, reassuring herself that he was around and supporting her. She asked, 'How did you get here first when you were behind me?'

He shrugged. 'I've always been a man for the back streets.'

'I believe you,' said Kate.

He could have been a street fighter, with that quick-moving quick-thinking toughness, but sometimes there was a stillness in him more powerful than action and more frightening.

Some time she might come up against the stillness, but now she said, 'Let's walk Baldy. I think there's a common along there.'

They walked up a grass-covered hill that looked down on the town, then they walked through the town. Then they ate, and it was another day of her holiday, but not carefree like the others had been. Mark was still fantastic company, he made her laugh and he made her talk, and she got the usual envious glances from women who would have changed places with her.

But today she was playing for time all the time. She did not want to get home early enough for company or phone calls. She had told Jenny she would be back today, and Jenny might have put the news around, but Kate felt that she would rather wait till tomorrow before facing the sympathetic concern of her friends.

For the rest of the journey she led the way, and the lights of Mark's car were never out of her driving mirror. They stopped her falling apart. She might well have done that, but she drew up dry-eyed in her home town with Mark coasting in behind.

This was a prosperous-looking road of tall Edwardian houses, their paintwork pristine, the windowsills edged with low wrought-iron balustrades, the pointed tops of front door porches elaborately carved.

Mark's eyebrows rose. 'Very impressive,' he remarked, and she grinned,

'I couldn't agree more, but it isn't mine. I live just off the town square, I don't have a garage, and I do have double yellow lines. I usually park in the square, but on Fridays I park in this road because there's a Saturday market and they start setting up stalls very early.'

She opened the boot to take out her luggage. 'Sorry about this, but it isn't far.'

A few minutes brought them to the bridge over the canal. Hers was the first of the row of terraced houses whose small back gardens had access gates to the towpath. There was no one on the towpath now, and a barge moored below was still and silent. Baldy showed an interest in the way down, Mark called him back, and Kate said, 'The canal's going to be a comedown for him after a seashore all to himself.'

'He's adaptable,' said Mark.

'We're here.' She put down cases and dug into her bag for her key. She liked her home very much. She had not been anxious to sell and move, and now she wouldn't have to. Her little home was a little security, but not all that much help when her whole world was cracking up.

She fumbled getting the key into the lock and said brightly, 'Not as impressive as the houses up the road.'

'I like it,' said Mark, 'and that's a handsome knocker.'

The door was dark blue that looked black in the lamplight, the brass knocker was a dolphin, and as Kate turned the key and pushed the door open she said, 'He was here when I came—he is nice, although I don't know what a dolphin is doing in the Midlands.'

After the vastness of the tower the tiny entrance hall seemed to close in on her, and she leaned against the wall while Mark brought in the baggage.

There was mail on the hall table. She pushed the envelopes around until Alan's writing leapt out at her. This had come through the post; he had not risked meeting her face to face, although the postmark was local. She left them all unopened and began switching on lights.

That didn't take long. Downstairs was a living-room the length of the house, a tiny cloakroom and a kitchen. It was cold, and she switched on the main room fire, both of her side lamps and a central light.

Almost at once the phone rang in the hall. Taking it off the cradle would have been her next move,

but as it was she had to answer; and although Mark
had followed her into the living-room he would not
have been able to avoid overhearing through the
open door.

'Hello,' said Kate.

'Is that you?' said Trish from over the way.

'I've just got back.'

'I wasn't expecting you till tomorrow, but I saw
lights go on.' Trish had been keeping watch on the
house while Kate was away, very conscientiously,
it seemed. Then she asked, 'Are you all right?' and
from her tone Trish knew what had been happening and what was waiting for Kate.

'Fine,' said Kate heartily. 'Really. But I am all
in—it was a long drive. I'll see you in the morning.'
She rang off and said, 'If it rings again let it, it's
too late for small talk.'

She was beginning to feel bone-weary. She drew
the curtains in the living-room, shutting out the
street. Mark was standing at the window overlooking her patio garden and under this low ceiling
he seemed taller than ever.

A stranger in her home. An unknown. It could
have been a mistake bringing him here. He domi-
nated this room just by standing there, and it was
too late now to start wondering if he might be less
likely to damp down a crisis than to spark off one
hell of a conflagration.

Kate heard her front door open, and Mark put
a hand on Baldy as Trish carolled, 'It's only me—
I've brought your key back.'

Kate reached the doorway into the hall. Trish was
wearing a yellow candlewick dressing-gown and
yellow slippers. Her face glistened with night cream
and there were three bendy curlers on the top of

her head. She was obviously ready for bed, but she said, 'I had to come over and see you were really all right. Oh, poor Kate, I've been ever so worried about you!'

Kate backed away, because Trish was advancing with open arms, ready for a comforting hug, and Kate wanted no hugging which would probably start her crying.

Trish followed, and got her first sidewards glimpse of Mark. It literally spun her round so that she was staring at him slack-jawed. Then she squealed, 'I didn't realise you had company!' and clapped her hand to her head. Shooting backwards into the hall, she mouthed at Kate, 'Why didn't you tell me? Why didn't you stop me?'

Kate's lips twitched. This was much better than being hugged and immeasurably preferable to being poor Kate. 'Sorry,' she mouthed herself, and Trish started to shake with silent giggles.

'See you tomorrow,' said Kate. 'Thanks for everything.'

'Who is he?' whispered Trish.

'Tomorrow,' said Kate.

'What? Oh yes, yes.' Trish was smiling now. In the open door to the street she whispered again, 'Don't tell him who I am—I'm going to look better next time!'

Kate went back into the living-room smiling, 'That's my very good neighbour.'

'So I gathered.'

'Here's a key for you.' Trish had dropped it on the hall table. 'I'm back at work on Monday, although we can still get around together.'

'I'm counting on it,' said Mark, and so was Kate. The object of this exercise was to give an impression of togetherness.

'I'll show you your room.' She went ahead up the little staircase. 'Bathroom,' she touched the door, 'and here you are.' The furniture was small and compact because this just missed being a boxroom, but there was a double bed.

'Guests get the bigger bed,' she said, 'but don't get any ideas,' and he shrugged his shoulders in mock innocence.

'What ideas? Did I make a pass?'

Never seriously. But until yesterday there had been Alan; she could no longer use that excuse.

Baldy was close to Mark, watching Kate. 'Where do you want him sleeping?' Mark asked.

'By the bed, on the bed—I don't mind.' The dog followed the man like his shadow, and she wondered, 'What happens when you're parted? Do you ever leave him behind?'

'When I do he knows I'll come back.'

'A touch of the Hettys,' she joked, but she thought, that must be nice for him.

Downstairs again she began to open her mail. Bills, circulars, letters. Two letters were from friends who wanted her to ring them as soon as she got back. That was in case she returned without knowing the score, and it was considerate of them.

But she did know, and when she was alone she would open Alan's letter and read what the man who had said he loved her had to say. She couldn't do that while Mark was watching her.

In the kitchen the fridge was almost empty. Trish would have been stocking up for her tomorrow, but in the morning Kate could shop for herself. There was coffee and tea, and she said, 'I came back early. Will you settle for a drink?'

'Of course.'

'I'll go up. I'll only be a few minutes in the bathroom.'

'Goodnight, Kate,' he said.

'You'll lock up, will you? You'll turn out the lights?'

'Of course.'

In her pretty little shell-pink bathroom Kate had a moment's time warp. Everything was the same in here, it seemed impossible that beyond that door nothing would ever be the same again. That Alan who always seemed so straight and so sincere had been cheating her.

She called down the stairs, 'Bathroom's all yours!' and closed her bedroom door and sat on the bed holding the square white envelope, in good quality stationery, a brand he always used for personal correspondence. Kate had had many a one, and they had all contained warm and loving words. The address was handwritten, he never used a typewriter, and seeing her name on an envelope in Alan's writing always gave her a tiny thrill.

Now she lifted the envelope to her lips. She had done that before, kissing before she opened and then settling down to read and starting to smile.

Only one page this time, paper that matched the envelope, his home address embossed top centre. And not 'My own darling,' but 'Dear Kate.'

This was one of the hardest letters he had ever had to write. They had been such good friends, he and Kate, and she was such a wonderful girl. But it was better, was it not, Kate, to face the truth that their relationship had reached a watershed. Friends they would always be, but——

She said softly, 'You stinking hypocrite,' and dropped the letter into a drawer in her dressing-table with the other matching envelopes.

He had been playing games with her: letting her try on his grandmother's ring, writing her love letters, making love to her. It had all been pretence, because it had never been Alan and Kate, secretly it had always been Alan and Celia.

Well, it could be Kate and Mark for a while. That would be something to soothe her pride. Mark was here; if she called him they could share the bigger bed. And anyone could see that he was experienced and skilful, and why not, for pity's sake?

It wouldn't be pity. He was attracted to her and she had invited him into her home and they were consenting adults. Natural and pleasurable, what more did she want?

But she felt so cold. Frigid was the word! The way she had for a long time after Philip had jilted her. If she lay naked beside Mark she would shrink from him, and he would know she was using him and walk away. He must not walk away, so that was no answer to the bitterness that was corroding her.

She opened her case and pulled out Alan's photograph. She covered it with the damp towelling bathrobe she had wrapped around her wet clothing, and placed it on a mock fur rug. That should deaden the sound. She didn't want Mark hearing breaking glass and coming in to investigate.

Then she found a shoe with a stiletto heel, metal-tipped, and brought it down again and again on the glass of the photograph until she must have pulverised it into a mass of razor-sharp splinters.

CHAPTER FOUR

NEXT morning, heavy-eyed from lack of sleep, Kate stepped over the bundle on the rug. Smashing the glass had released some of her frustration last night; his photograph had been a substitute for Alan's smug face. But she had not slept much easier for hitting out.

By morning light the gesture seemed stupid. It was not going to worry Alan, who would never know, but it would be impossible to get all the glass slivers out of her robe, and she would have to be careful they didn't spill on to the rug to draw blood if she walked barefoot.

She had done no other unpacking, and now she went about that task, putting clothes in wardrobe and drawers, piling the sea-damp items together. Harry the Horse came out of the case tangled again; he had a talent for getting into a twist. But as she held him up he did a slow twirl, round and round, ending on unravelled strings.

'Thank you,' she said idiotically, and slipped the rings on the end of the curtain rail. He hung there, looking the picture of dejection.

When she chose him she had thought he was cute, but she had been happy herself then and his mournful expression had been funny. 'I suppose you couldn't manage a smile,' she said, and was thankful that no one could hear her.

The house was still when she put her head out of her bedroom door, and she went quietly down the stairs. The curtains had not been drawn in the living-room, so Mark and Baldy must still be asleep, and she ran upstairs again to collect the bathrobe and the smashed photograph and take them out to the bin.

Her little walled patio was flagstoned and brightened with terracotta pots and troughs, although the only colours now were a few winter pansies and the last of the pink geraniums. During the hot summer she had brought out the sun-loungers and served al fresco meals. Friends had sometimes joined her, but the best times had been alone with Alan.

Right now if she closed her eyes she could imagine it was summer again and he was here, relaxing as if this backyard were a wonderful garden and sharing it with Kate made everything perfect. But all through those drowsy sunny hours he must have been thinking of Celia, resenting having to keep away from her while they angled for her father's approval.

How long would it be before Kate could be out here, or in her home, without seeing Alan everywhere, remembering what he said, what they did, knowing now that all of it had been a lie?

She could not imagine summer. It would always be winter. She was clutching the bathrobe, feeling the shape of the frame inside it. She lifted the lid of the bin and dropped the bundle into the bag, as the gate opened and Mark and Baldy walked in.

Kate jumped as guiltily as if she had been caught getting rid of a body and gasped, 'How long have you been up?'

'An hour or so. We've been walking the towpath; we got as far as the second lock.'

'The back door was still bolted.'

'We went out through the front door.' He had a key, and for a few seconds she looked at him. No eye contact, she was still wary of that, but his presence and personality were vigorous enough to clear away the shadows. While Mark was around she could look at him and she wouldn't see Alan.

She said, 'I'll get us some breakfast. If you'll make the coffee I'll be back in a few minutes.'

She slipped into a coat that was hanging in the hall closet, and wished she had worn this on Thursday when she walked into the sea, and that she still had her lovely cashmere. She tied her hair back with a scarf, she must wash it as soon as she got back, then she grabbed a shopping bag and headed for a small grocers a few minutes' walk away.

At the end of her road early shoppers were thronging the market, and that was where Kate would be meeting people she knew. There wouldn't be many who had not heard the gossip about Alan Foster and Celia Chambers, but when Kate ran that gauntlet Mark would be with her.

Now she reached the shop and made some quick purchases and got out again without any hassle. As she turned into her road a girl pushing a pram called across, 'Hi, Kate,' and Kate waved and called a cheery, 'Hello,' back. Then she strode off and let herself in through her front door.

Mark was in the little galley of a kitchen. Alan was clumsy in this confined space so that Kate had always found it less trouble to prepare meals and clear away herself. But Mark moved easily, wasting no effort, taking the loaf from her, putting slices in the toaster, and she said, 'Mind your elbows, my kitchen's rather cramped after the tower.'

'I've been in tighter fits,' he said.

'Smaller than this? I didn't think they came any smaller, except maybe a caravan or a boat.' She laughed. 'Or a cell.'

His answering smile was quick and she had the impression of something she was not sharing. Then he told her, 'Jenny phoned. Will you ring her back? She said it was urgent.'

'It would be, with Jenny.' Now Mark had answered it certainly would be, and she went back into the hall, closing the kitchen door. Later in the morning she would be seeing Jenny in the office; she might be on her way there now, but as she had phoned Kate would try to get her at home.

She did not really want to play this game. She doubted if she had the stamina for going around with a smile on her face when she felt like death. But she dialled Jenny's home number and Jenny answered on the second ring. 'I was just going to try you again,' said Jenny as soon as Kate spoke. 'Who was that?'

'A very good friend,' said Kate.

'Sexy voice,' said Jenny.

'You should see the rest of him.' The door was shut, but she still spoke softly.

'Do I know him?'

'Not yet,' said Kate, and hung up. That had to do Jenny for now; she could be relied on to relay that to Kate's colleagues, and when Kate turned up with Mark she had to look good and without a care in the world.

She opened the kitchen door, pulling the scarf off her head. I've got to wash my hair again, it's still like seaweed.'

'That's what comes of diving off causeways,' said Mark.

'Very true.'

She washed and conditioned it, and went down with a towel wrapped around her head because she was gasping for coffee. The kitchen had only working space and Mark had carried a tray to the table by the patio window. He sat there now with a local guidebook he had taken from her shelves. 'If you haven't anything planned for this morning,' Kate said, 'would you like to walk round our market?'

He said he would and she left it at that, while he read the guidebook and she ate her toast. Until the phone rang again and she got up reluctantly to answer it. It would have been ringing whether she had brought Mark back or not. If she had been there alone the callers would have stammered what they had to say, because a public jilting was such a savage thing. Her friends would have been indignant for her and sorry for her and thankful in their hearts that it was not happening to them.

But now Trish came over sounding quite gleeful, no pity there. 'So who *is* he?' she demanded.

'The man I've been on holiday with,' said Kate softly, and Trish whooped. 'Really? Go on, then,' followed by a crash and a howl and a scream. 'I'll call you back,' said Trish. 'They're fighting again,' and Kate just had time to gabble,

'Don't ring, it's not easy to talk. I'll get over some time,' before Trish hurried off to separate her continually scrapping sons.

After that Kate replaced the receiver slightly askew; she didn't want any more calls. Upstairs she blew her hair dry until it shone in a smooth bouncing bob. She was looking quite bouncing herself, with colour on her cheekbones and lips curved ready to smile.

Now she must face them. She called, 'Ready to go?' as she came down the stairs, and went into the kitchen to collect her shopping bag.

Funny how little things affected you when you were punch-drunk. Harry the Horse's gloomy depressing face, and on the shopping bag the marmalade kitten with its Cheshire Cat grin. She had never noticed before how blank its eyes were, and she thought, that's me, with a false grin on my face.

Mark came into the hall. In leather jacket, dark trousers and dark rollneck sweater, his tall lean body and hawkish face spelled style. The lazy, usually amused voice was a turn-on too, and if Kate needed an attractive man to flaunt around town Thaddeus Mark Brandon was ideal for her purpose.

When he put a light arm round her shoulders there was a smothering, pounding sensation in her chest, and instinctively she ducked her head. But he was not kissing her. She heard him breathe in above her head, then he said cheerfully, 'Not a trace of seaweed left.'

'I should hope not, I use a good conditioner.' She smiled brightly. 'Shall we go?'

He put the phone straight on its cradle while she registered surprise. 'I suppose I must have done that after that last call,' she said.

'Is there anything you want to miss?'

He was suggesting she had done it on purpose, and she had. 'Plenty,' she said. 'That's the trouble with phones, you can't ignore them.' There had not been a phone in the tower, but his phone, of course, would be in the shop.

'I could do an answering service for you.' He said in fruity theatrical tones, 'This is the Kershaw residence, madam is unavailable at the moment, may I ask who is calling?'

She laughed, 'There's class! You don't come across a lot of butlers these days.'

The square was filled with rows of stalls and swarming with shoppers. A bandstand, dating from times when brass bands played on high days and holidays, stood in the centre of the square. Sometimes a restaurant put tables and chairs out, but now stalls were set up there too and everywhere was busy and bustling.

Buildings around the square still had a Victorian façade although inside most of them had changed out of recognition. There were shops, offices, including that of the county newspaper, a few private houses, and strolling between the stalls Kate saw familiar faces and smiled when they saw her.

So far she was managing to dodge those who would have stopped to talk, and when a woman came out of a boutique calling 'Kate!' she hurried away. Mark was rooting through the boxes on a secondhand bookstall, and Kate came back to him as soon as Ilse was back in her own shop. Then she bought fruit and vegetables, filling her bag and handing it over to him when he reached for it.

For a dog used to wide open spaces Baldy behaved well in crowds, keeping at Mark's heels, ears back. He looked under control but not be trifled with, and Kate noticed that nobody tried to pet him.

When they came to the old chapel she said, 'Here's where I work.' The sign above the big open doors read 'Radio Danilo' and the extensions behind more than trebled its size. 'Would you like to see round?'

She willed him to say yes, but he said, 'Later, maybe.'

Going in this morning and saying her piece might take the heat off her for a while. 'I have to go in,' she said, and when she got no response to that she asked, 'Will you wait for me? I'll only be a few minutes.'

'Of course.'

She took a deep breath as she walked into the foyer. Once past the open doors there were no signs left of the old chapel. This was in every sense a hive of modern technology.

From behind the long reception desk a woman blinked through big round spectacles when she saw Kate and called, 'Have a nice holiday?' realising as soon as she had spoken that she might have been tactless.

Kate beamed and said, 'The best ever. Wait till you see what I brought back!'

The top of the stairs led directly into the huge newsroom that Kate shared with other journalists. Beyond glass panels was one of the broadcasting studios. A red light showed and a man was speaking into microphones. Another glass-panelled section was the news editor's office, and Kate's desk, with its VDU, was one of two rows of identical workplaces.

As Kate walked in some of the talking stopped. Most of her colleagues looked towards her, and the girl who was nearest came to meet her. Jenny was the news editor's secretary, so all the women would know by now that a very good friend of Kate's had answered her phone this morning.

All the same Nicola, with whom Kate had shared confidences, asked anxiously, 'All right?'

'Never better,' said Kate. 'I'm still on leave till Monday, but I looked in to see if there was any mail for me.'

Nicola was trying to work out if Kate was putting on a brave face, because she knew how Kate felt about Alan Foster and that he had treated her abominably.

Kate opened the top drawer and went through her mail. Office matters would have to be dealt with, personal letters usually went home. There was not much here, and there was no big square envelope with Alan's writing on it. She had checked that in seconds, although he would not be writing to the studios; he would not be writing to her at all.

Then Jenny, having spotted her through the glass panels and come haring out, grabbed her elbow, hissing, 'Who *is* he?'

Kate lifted her head and faced her friends. 'His name's Mark Brandon, and I met him when I was looking for somewhere to stay.' She smiled as if she was recalling something incredible. 'We sort of clicked right away and—well, I stayed with him and things got better and better, and now he's spending a few days with me.'

She could not have carried on like this if Mark had come into the office with her. She was telling no lies; they had clicked, there had been a rapport. But if he had been standing beside her she could hardly have smouldered like the panting beauty queen in the studio photograph, giving the impression that all had been steamingly sexual from the start.

Nicola gulped, 'You mean——?' Then she asked, 'Did you know about Alan and Celia before?'

Kate pulled a knowing face that could have meant anything, except her real feelings of bitter betrayal, and Nicola gasped, 'So you were cooling off as well?'

She had been really bothered for Kate. They had all been shocked, and now it seemed they had been worrying over nothing. Kate had not been crazy about Alan Foster after all, she had never come in here smiling like the cat with the cream over him. Nicola felt she might have dropped a hint, and said quite sharply, 'That's a lucky coincidence.'

'It's a funny old world,' said Kate, and Nicola wondered if there was a wistfulness in that and decided that of course she was glad Kate had found someone else.

'So where is he?' she asked.

'Waiting for me.' Kate looked down from the window with her female co-workers grouped behind her. 'The man with the dog.'

There were appreciative murmurs as Mark looked up and Kate waved and he waved back. 'Very tasty,' Nicola decided.

'Very much to my taste,' Kate grinned. 'And I'm thinking of accepting joint custody of the dog. See you.' She went as if she had wings on her feet and she knew that they watched for her to run out through the doors below and across to Mark. She had intended to walk away, arm in arm with him, making him smile by telling him that she had told Jenny he was a tall dark no-name stranger she had picked up on holiday.

But when she reached him he held up another puppet that he had just bought from the charity

stall—a cow with long painted eyelashes and a
smirk. 'A friend for Harry,' he said. 'I thought she
might cheer him up,' and that would have made her
laugh even if there had been no audience.

'When I hung him up this morning he looked so
mournful,' she said. 'I could kiss you for Harry.'
Her lips brushed his cheek and they both knew it
meant nothing, but that was not the impression the
onlookers got, watching Kate and her 'lover'
strolling away together.

They left the market, walking back up Kate's
road towards where they had parked their cars last
night. As they reached Trish's house Kate said, 'I've
got to look in here. I'll follow you, it's another brief
call.'

She caught Trish alone. On Saturday morning
her husband had taken the twins to the park and
Trish was hurrying around tidying up after them.
When she saw Kate her eyes brightened. Kate was
never boring, and what was happening to her now
was riveting.

Trish was very willing to leave the bedmaking and
sit over coffee, but Kate said, 'I have to dash, we're
going off somewhere, but I know you want to know
the score. You've heard about Alan and Celia?'
Trish nodded, sober-faced. 'Well, that's fine by me,'
said Kate. 'She's welcome to him. I met Mark while
I was on holiday. He's a photographer, he's got a
little shop and he's very good. You'll like him—
you'll be meeting him.'

There was no way of avoiding that, Trish was
nodding again; and Kate stayed for a few more
minutes, thanking Trish for looking after the house,
checking that all was well with Trish's family,
sounding natural and smiling a lot.

At the door Trish asked, 'It is all right, isn't it? I mean, this isn't just a rebound?' and Kate looked at her steadily and said quietly and clearly,

'Believe me, I've never been happier.'

She was lying, but it reassured Trish, wiping the doubt from her face and her voice. 'That's *smashing*!' She giggled, 'Wasn't it awful, me barging in in my curlers? You say he's a photographer; I wonder if he'd do the twins? I'd pay him, of course, but I was thinking of a photograph for them to give Simon for his birthday and it might be nice to have it taken at home.'

'I'll ask,' Kate promised. She saw no reason why Mark should turn down a commission, nor why she should mention that the twins could be holy horrors. Awkward subjects must be one of the risks of the job, and it would be interesting to see if Mark could handle them.

He was sitting in his car reading a morning paper. As he leaned across to open the passenger door for her the dog lumbered over into the back seat, accepting the inevitable, and Kate said, 'Baldy, you're a gentleman,' and scratched the top of his sleek dark head.

'You've bought a paper,' she said to Mark. 'I thought you weren't interested in world affairs.'

He folded it and slipped it under the seat. 'Even my head comes out of the sand eventually,' he said. He sounded as if he was joking, but she wished that holiday could have lasted longer, where no phones rang and they were alone even in the middle of crowds.

Today they drove around the neighbourhood buying food, but mainly sightseeing where he might return and photograph at his leisure while Kate was working. They had lunch and tea in attractive hostelries, and arrived back in the early evening. By then the market had cleared from the square, Kate collected her car and drove down behind Mark to park it in its usual spot nearer the house and handy for the office.

The phone was ringing when she opened the front door, and she grimaced as she answered it and recognised Ilse cooing, 'Hello, Kate.' Ilse Peters was not among her favourite people. She always looked like a glossy magazine model—running one of the best dress shops in town, so she should—and she had a gushing line in sympathy that hid her delight in other people's troubles.

If you had any sense at all you were careful what you told Ilse. She was a fair-weather friend, and Kate was sure that when she heard about Alan and Celia she had reminded everybody about Philip. 'Oh, *poor* Kate,' Kate could imagine her saying. 'This is the second time she's been jilted. Is she just unlucky, or what?'

Now she was saying, 'I'm having a little party this evening, I do hope you can get along,' with a little trill of laughter. 'Bring along the mystery man, of course.'

Taking Mark to one of Ilse's 'do's would give him maximum local coverage, but Kate was not sure she was ready for that. She asked, 'Could I leave it at maybe?' and Ilse said coyly,

'They all think he's very handsome.'

'Do they?' said Kate as she hung up.

Not really, she thought. Alan is handsome with regular features, but Mark has the devil's hungry look, and if he goes to your party tonight he'll surely stir up something.

She said, 'That was an invitation for both of us—
a party. The food will be cordon bleu because it
always is. How do you feel about it?'

'Not me,' he said promptly. 'I'm not a social
animal. You go and enjoy your supper.'

She would have thought he would be terrific in
company, a natural charmer who could talk and
listen, but his refusal was pretty emphatic. And it
might have been to avoid an argument that he took
Baldy out for a walk along the towpath, leaving
Kate to make her own decision.

She could hardly arrive at Ilse's alone. If she
couldn't persuade Mark to accompany her she
wouldn't go. If she did go it would be an ordeal,
but it would show Ilse and her guests that nobody
need feel sorry for Kate, and on the whole she supposed she ought to turn up. If she could just get
Mark to change his mind.

So she would start to get ready, then she would
come downstairs and Mark would be back from
walking the dog, and she would say, 'Do come with
me. It'll be more fun than sitting here all evening,
and we can cadge some leftovers for Baldy.' When
he saw the trouble she had gone to—he had never
seen her in full glamour—he would surely give in.

She took out one of her favourites, a black sequinned sheath dress with a diagonal neckline
baring one shoulder. Mark was taking his time,
unless they had come back and she hadn't heard
them. She had put on her gleaming party face, fixed
her hair, and was slipping in the second long jet
and gold earring when the phone rang.

It was Nicola. 'Kate? Ilse says you're coming tonight. And I'll bet she didn't mention it, but Alan
and Celia are, and if you weren't expecting to see

them it could be awkward, so I thought you ought
to know.'

Ilse would be expecting some excitement there,
and Kate thanked heaven for her friends. She said,
'Bless you,' and then, 'I didn't say we would, and
as it happens we've just decided we'd prefer a cosy
evening in.'

Nicola was not sure if this was a change of plan,
but she said gaily, 'From what I saw of him I don't
blame you! 'Bye for now, then.'

'Have fun at Ilse's,' said Kate, and Nicola
laughed,

'Not as much fun as she was hoping. She'll be
disappointed. Can I mention Mark to Alan?'

'Why not?' said Kate. 'Ilse will.' She laughed too
until the connection was broken off, but then she
went into the living-room and sat down, shaking
like a leaf, feeling the blood draining out of her
face.

She should have guessed that Alan might be invited, and now she knew what a confrontation with
him could do to her. It was one thing being bright
for friends, but seeing Alan and Celia together,
while the pain was still raw, would blow her fragile
defences. Even if she steeled herself to carry it off,
and fooled them all, she would not fool Mark. He
would realise how vulnerable she was if she walked
into Ilse's drawing-room and found Alan and Celia
there.

Ilse was a mischief-maker. She would not have
warned Alan either. It would have been embarrassing for him and Celia, but they were the
winners. Kate was the loser, and if she had turned
white and started shaking, the way she was now

just thinking about it, she would have been 'poor Kate' for ever.

She walked up and down the living-room until she stopped shaking and the colour came back into her cheeks. Now she had to get out of her finery, and she would take a drink upstairs with her so that by the time she came down again her nerves would have steadied.

She was at the corner cabinet where she kept her few bottles when Baldy bounded into the room, and she moved away quickly before Mark could follow him. She always seemed to be hopping with guilt when he caught her unawares, and although she had every right to be pouring her own drink in her own house secret drinking might call for an explanation.

He stood in the doorway, watching her, then he said, 'You look sensational. There won't be another woman there tonight who can hold a candle to you.'

Kate blushed with pleasure, although it was not true. She had not been sensational enough to keep Alan loving her. But Mark's admiration boosted her confidence so that she wondered for a moment if she could face Alan so long as Mark was with her.

She said slowly, 'You haven't had second thoughts about going to the party?' and was relieved when he said no, as decisively as he had the first time.

'Well, I have,' she said, 'I've been thinking. It would be a long night and I don't really want to go. I was just going to get this off and get back into something sloppier.'

'That would be a waste,' he said. 'Shall we dine out, in style?'

There were places locally where diners dressed
for dinner, where the prices were ridiculous and
sometimes the food was good. She had eaten in
most of them, usually with Alan, but now she said,
'Or shall we stay in, in style? I can set out a pretty
table with wine and candlelight, and we can eat
from today's shopping.'

'No, I'll see to the food. You lay the table.'

He was closing the front door behind him before
she could ask, 'What are you getting?' and she
opened the gateleg table, moving it to the centre of
the room. Then she put long white candles in crystal
holders, and laid two placemats with her rosewood-
handled cutlery and the white gold-rimmed plates.

Ready for a bottle of wine she was chilling, she
brought out two antique glasses that Alan had given
her on her last birthday. Until now she had only
used them with him, but tonight she would share
them with Mark. Alan could keep her gifts, she
wanted nothing back, and she told herself that these
were just glasses now, pretty possessions but
meaning no more to her than anything else on the
table.

When they turned off the lights and lit the candles
it would look festive and intimate, and she smiled
at her reflection in the hall mirror, remembering
Mark's words and his expression of wholehearted
approval.

It would have been hellish at Ilse's with everyone
weighing her up against Celia and some of them
deciding that Alan had chosen the right girl.
Compared with that, an evening alone with an attractive man who had just told her she was gorgeous would be bliss. And whatever they ate would

taste better than Ilse's haute cuisine, because that would have choked her.

She picked up the new puppet from the hall table and took it up to her room. 'Company for you, Harry,' she said, and shoved him along the curtain rail to make room for another set of rings.

When Mark went away the puppets would be left hanging here, and if she didn't break the habit she might still be talking to them. Cold comfort, she thought; but where would she look for comfort when Mark went away? And she heard the front door open and called, 'Mark, is that you?'

'How many keys have you handed out?'

'Oh, dozens,' she said airily. Only the one he had. 'I'm introducing Harry to what's-her-name.' He came up the stairs and into her room, and she pointed them out. 'There they are. Don't they make a good pair?'

But he was looking away from the puppets when he said, 'I'm beginning to think they do,' and the long cheval mirror framed him and Kate like a picture. She was stunning in her shining dress and earrings and her glam make-up. He was casually dressed, understated, but when she met his eyes in the mirror her breath caught, and as her bare shoulder brushed his jacket sleeve she felt a tiny electric shock. Maybe she was not frigid after all, but going overboard because she was lonely would be just as destructive.

She said lightly, 'No doubt about it, we'd be a knockout at any party. What shall we call Harry's friend?'

'Clarabelle?'

'How about Ilse?' That was a joke to keep to herself. She said blandly, 'I know a cow called Ilse,' and without giving him time to ask about that she asked him, 'So what are we having for dinner?'

Choice had been limited: fish and chips, the pizza parlour and the Chinese takeaway. Even the delicatessen had been closed, and in the hall was a large white carrier bag from the Chinese takeaway. 'Lovely,' said Kate. 'Absolutely my first choice.'

'And this,' said Mark, picking up a bottle of champagne. 'It's chilled, I got it from a hotel. Will you dish up while I wash? I can't match you for elegance, but I can change my shirt.'

'I'm sure you'll look devastating,' she joked, 'by candlelight.'

She emptied the half-dozen tinfoil containers into dishes, the prawns and the bamboo shoots, the chicken in lemon sauce, beansprouts and cashew nuts and mushrooms, crabmeat and sweetcorn. It was colourful and it smelt appetising, and she lit the candles and turned out the main lights with Baldy sprawled full length in the glow from the electric fire.

Mark turned out the hall light as he reached the bottom of the stairs, and came from the shadows into the room where Kate had just seated herself at the table. He was wearing a white shirt, open at the neck, and she thought, no wonder you get on so well with the gypsies, you could be a blood brother.

He sat opposite her, and the candlelight flickered in his dark eyes. Light from the campfire, she thought, and he asked, 'Why are you smiling?'

She told him the truth when she could. 'I was thinking you look like a gypsy and we could be round a campfire.'

'Not the way you're dressed.'

'Not even my golden earrings?' She turned her head so that her hair swung bell-like and the long earrings swayed against her cheeks.

'Pretty,' he said, and if he had touched an earring they might have kissed across the table, and that would have been pleasant but dangerous, so she was glad he did not.

She began to help herself to the food and they consulted each other over dishes. They had been eating meals together for a fortnight. By now she knew as much about his culinary tastes as she knew about anyone's. Alan was a fussy eater, but Mark tackled most things cheerfully.

When her plate was piled she said, 'It ought to be chopsticks.'

'Can you use chopsticks?' he asked.

'I've tried, from time to time. I'm better with a fork.'

'I'll teach you,' he said.

'Good at it, are you?'

'Very good.' He grinned wickedly. 'Some time, dear Kate, I hope to show you just how good I can be.' Chopsticks had nothing to do with this, but they were only fooling, although when he stood up she held her breath. 'And it's about time I started taking some pictures of you,' he said.

He went to fetch his camera and she let the held breath out again. Of course she was not disappointed that he was not trying to make love to her, but it was no compliment him taking pictures to take away with him. Something to remind him of a girl who had not made enough impression to live on in his mind, let alone in his heart.

Her own heart was a closed shop, but he was vivid enough in her mind to leave an indelible

image. She would need no photograph to remember how he looked, and that was depressing,
because she already had enough lonely memories
to last a lifetime.

She reached for the champagne bottle and something sharp and sparkling to recapture her party
mood, tearing off the foil top and unwinding the
wire over the cork. Then slowly and steadily she
eased up the cork, releasing it with a loud and ex-
plosive force.

The wine foamed like a fountain, and Baldy
screamed and streaked from the room like a bat
out of hell. In the hall he cannoned into Mark, and
Kate ran out after him. The cork must have hit him
in the eye, done some sort of agonising damage.
Now he was howling, head thrown back, and Mark
was holding him, talking gently. 'Easy, boy, easy,
it's all right.'

'Oh, God, what's happened? Where's he hurt?'
Kate demanded.

'It was the noise,' said Mark. 'It sounded like
gunshot.'

The animal's eyes were wild, but the howling had
become a panting and now he was shivering. Kate
stood still and quiet, until Baldy staggered back to
the fire and lay there, tongue lolling, giving the
sheepish impression of someone who has made a
fool of himself. Then she said, '*Gunshot*?'

Mark took her hand and ran it under the animal's ribcage, and she felt the weal of extensive
scar tissue. It was long healed so that it was no
longer even tender, but he must have suffered terribly, and she whispered, 'Oh, you poor love, how
did it happen—was it an accident?' From the man's
face she knew it was not, and she said, 'Don't tell

me how, but how cruel, how awful! Do bangs always terrify him?'

She had knocked her chair sidewards when she rushed out after the dog. Mark picked it up and she sat down. It was a wonder she hadn't knocked over the bottle too, but that was upright, and he poured into the two glasses. 'Hardly ever,' he said. 'Time was when a car backfiring could have sent him running for miles, but now he'll give an ear twitch and that's it. Popping corks he can take too. This one must have taken him by surprise. He was probably asleep.'

'Having a nightmare?' she wondered, and promised, 'I won't do it again. I'll wake him before I explode anything else.'

Mark grinned. 'He's a liability, isn't he?'

'No, he isn't. He's brave and beautiful, and I'm glad I've met him.'

'I'm glad you've met him too,' said Mark.

During the evening he took some photographs of her, and she entered into the spirit of it. She was quite photogenic and of course it didn't mean he would have forgotten her without a picture to remind him. He was glad he had met her, and dining in style was definitely a success.

As the candles burned lower he took another picture. The others had been party shots, tossing back her hair, smiling over a forkful of food, laughing at something he was saying. Now he said, 'Look at me, Kate,' and she joked,

'I've been looking at you all evening.'

But this time he did not smile, and her eyelids half closed and she smiled with closed lips. 'Thank you,' he said, and she said,

'That's not going to be up to much.'

'We'll see.'

She might ask him now about photographing the twins. She had been thinking about that and wondering if it was a good idea. Last year when Trish took them to a local studio they had both seized on the same toy and the photographs had been disastrous. She said, 'You do child studies, don't you? There were some good ones in the shop. My neighbour over the way asked me if you'd take a photograph of hers for her husband's birthday.' She admitted, starting to grin, 'The trouble is they're very active. It would be like photographing a wagonload of monkeys.'

'Strewth,' he said. 'How many are there?'

'Two. Twins.'

'Two monkeys I should be able to handle.'

'I'll come back in my lunch hour and take you over,' she said.

'I'm going to need back-up?' She laughed, but she would go over with him, because she didn't want Trish telling him how lovely it was to see Kate in love again.

It was after midnight when they cleared the table. She tied an apron over her dress and slipped on yellow rubber gloves, and he whisked through the stacked dishes with a tea-towel. It would only take a few minutes, and the remains would have been revolting to come down to in the morning.

This was her best china. She would have been sorry to break any of it, although any piece could have been replaced, but the item that shot through her soapy fingers was a wine-glass. It hit the sink and shattered, and instinctively she gave an anguished cry, 'Oh, *no*—oh, not *that*!'

It was beautiful and it was irreplaceable, and this seemed part of the chaos that her life was in. Breaking things: her heart, the photograph, the slender-stemmed goblet. Her control was only skin-deep yet and she could not pretend that it didn't matter. The muscles in her face clenched, and she stood with tight shut eyes holding back tears.

When she looked at him Mark was looking at her. She couldn't tell him that this had been Alan's gift. It had to be enough that it was a lovely old glass that she had treasured, and she said, 'It was old.' He could see that. 'Like a family heirloom. My grandmother's,' she invented wildly, and that was pure invention, because her parents' parents had died before she was old enough to remember them and her family had had no heirlooms.

She turned back to the bowl, and he put a hand on her bare shoulder so that she whirled round again, and shut her eyes as though he would read her mind and know that it had come from a man who had been her lover.

He ran a thumb along her cheekbone, so that she felt it against the lashes and knew it came away wet, and he said impatiently, 'For heaven's sake, Katy, don't weep for a broken glass!'

She should have said she was not weeping. Instead she snapped, 'Oh, shut up, I'll cry if I want to,' and then the smile that his slow grin always evoked tugged at her lips. 'Ah well,' she said, 'I've still got one glass left.'

'And if you feel that you must cry I've got two shoulders, you're welcome to either of them.'

'I'll take a rain-check.' She was smiling without effort now, and they finished the clearing away and said goodnight to each other. And as she got out of her glamour and ready for bed she wondered, not for the first and not for the last time, if an affair with Mark would make or break her.

CHAPTER FIVE

SUNDAY, the last day of Kate's holiday, they went to Castle Fort. High in the hills, it had been an Iron Age fort. The pattern of huge early rings was still visible, and all year round it was popular with visitors. The nearby pub was well known for its food and its comfortable atmosphere, and Kate had eaten here several times with Alan.

It had not rained since she came home. Today the weather was cold and dry, and they walked with the dog, round the rings and over the heath, then returned to the pub for lunch.

The woman behind the bar smiled at Kate and asked, 'Is Mr Foster with you?'

'Not today,' said Kate. Not any more. Come to that, he never was with her, not even when they had strolled in here together and sat down side by side. But Mark gave the ones who recognised her something to think about, and Kate left with her fingers slipped through his arm.

Again it was late when they got home. She was tired and due at work in the morning. She was going to miss being with Mark all day long, but it was a good start to the day, breakfasting with him and Baldy, and they walked with her to the square, towards her office and his car.

After work the staff often dropped into a wine bar, to gossip, to discuss the day's stories, some to eat. Kate told Mark this, pointing out George and

Gina's, and suggested, 'Shall we meet in there, around six o'clock?'

'I don't know where I'll be. I'll see you back at the house.'

'Fine.' She would go straight home.

They reached his car. He opened the door and Baldy jumped into the front seat, and several of Kate's co-workers were walking along the pavement. 'Take care,' she said, looking up at Mark, and he put a hand under her chin, and kissed her cheek.

'You too,' he said. 'Keep out of the water.'

She hoped the kiss had been noted, as she hurried across to the old chapel still feeling the cool light touch of his lips and fingers.

They were waiting for her with more questions, like what did he do for a living? and she told them about the photography studio at the seaside, and that this was his slack time during which he free-lanced. Yes, he was staying with her. Of *course* in the spare room; but she said that with dancing eyes so that nobody believed her.

'How did the party go?' she asked Nicola, who grinned,

'Oh, so-so. Ilse told Alan you'd come back with someone you met on holiday. Very macho, she said. Alan seemed taken aback.' That was balm to Kate's pride, and when Nicola enquired, 'And how was the cosy evening for two?' she breathed ecstatically,

'*Very* cosy!'

'So when are we going to meet him?'

'Give me a break,' said Kate. 'It's early days and I don't want to share him.'

Mark was not anxious to meet any of them. On the contrary. And if he stayed a mystery man they would accept Kate's version of the relationship. She looked and sounded like a girl who was happy and fulfilled, and as long as they went on believing that they would never suspect how cruelly she had been hurt.

'Morning, Kate,' boomed the news editor. 'Come back to work, have we, or are we holding a meeting?'

From then on Kate had no time for anything but work. As a roving reporter she went out to interview villagers in a local beauty spot, who were threatened with a mini-town development in the fields around them. In the studio she edited that down to the allotted length of programme time, wrote and recorded her introduction and tailpiece, and answered a couple of letters that were waiting for her.

It was a typical busy day, and at the end of it she enjoyed saying, 'I have to get home,' and hurrying off. When she passed Mark's car that quickened her step, because it meant he was back already, and she let herself into the hall calling, 'I'm home!'

Baldy welcomed her, not effusively, but he came wagging his tail, and Mark said, 'That's what I like to hear. The breadwinner returns.'

'Have you had a fun day?' Kate hung her coat in the closet. 'Taken any good photographs?'

'No, but I've met some funny people.'

'Where have you been?'

She nearly always came back to an empty house. She never minded; you threw a few switches and there was light and the red glow of the fire. Sometimes she had friends staying, but none of them had seemed so at home in her little house. It

felt so right to find Mark waiting here that she could
have been sharing a home with him for years. She
went to him smiling and asked again, 'Where *have*
you been?'

'Antique centres, shops.'

'I didn't know you were into antiques.' There
were none in the tower, and during their two weeks'
roaming the nearest they had come to the old and
rare on sale had been the Barn, and that was mostly
cheerful junk. Mark photographed 'anything over
two hundred years old', but that was a different
matter.

'I was, today,' he said. 'They're not an exact
match, but they're the same period, early Victorian
and almost the same style.'

Two wineglasses stood on her sideboard, with
slender twisted stems in faintly smoky glass. 'Now
there are three,' he said. 'You can entertain. Maybe
they're not your family heirlooms, but they
probably belonged to somebody's grandmother.'

Kate was overwhelmed, it was such a thoughtful
thing to do for her. She picked one up, shaking her
head in wonderment. 'They're beautiful,' she said
huskily. 'I'll take such care of them, I'll never wash
these in rubber gloves.' She put it down very carefully, and clasped her hands behind his head so that
she was leaning against him. 'Thank you very
much.'

He said quietly, 'I don't think you'd better do
that, Katy.'

If it was not the beat of his heart she was hearing
it must be the throbbing in her own blood, and she
was suddenly acutely conscious of his hard body
and the shape and texture of his face. The skin,
smooth and brown, the dark straight brows, the

long mouth only a breath away from her mouth. And the eyes that she still could not read and still could not meet.

If he kissed her now he would make full sensual love to her. They would no longer be platonic friends and she would be a hostage to fate again. She wanted no more of that. She unclasped her hands and managed a dazzling smile and said, 'That was a thank-you, not a turn-on. Now, tell me about the funny folk you met today and I'll tell you about the farmer I met who's going to let a very fierce bull loose if the developers move into his ten-acre field.'

They stayed home that evening, and Mark did a hilarious mimicry of dealers he had dealt with in his search for lookalike glasses, from deadly serious types to rampant eccentrics. It was as good as a cabaret turn, and Kate went over her interviews for him. He could hear them again over the air to-morrow afternoon in *What are the Planners Up to Now?*

'And I should be able to get away for an hour at midday,' she said. 'Would you see what you can do about Trish's twins?'

So next day they went over to Trish's, and again Kate watched the reaction she had come to expect. Trish, who was faithful and loving and thought Simon her husband looked like Richard Gere although nobody else did, giggled like a starstruck schoolgirl when she was introduced to Mark.

The twins were let loose while Trish and Kate ate cheese and chutney sandwiches in the kitchen. Trish wanted to know more than Kate intended to tell, but Kate managed to make it sound like a love story without actually inventing anything. Because they had met by chance and been inseparable ever since, and he was sexy and smashing and Kate did think a lot of him.

After about half an hour Mark announced that he had his pictures. The twins were grinning, which was not a good sign, but so was Mark, and when Trish asked apprehensively, 'Did they behave? How did you manage?' he said,

'I let them rip and caught them in flight.'

'I hope they come out.' Trish was apologising in advance because she had been very embarrassed when she'd collected the last studio photographs.

'I'm sure they will,' Mark said.

'Would you both like to come over for supper?' Trish thought Simon would like to meet Mark, and Kate was always welcome. But Kate looked at Mark and knew he was about to refuse, and said, 'Thanks, but we can't manage tonight. Some other time?'

'Yes, of course,' said Trish, and managed to whisper to Kate as they left, 'I can see why you're keeping him to yourself!' Which was what Kate did for most of that week.

They spent their evenings together, they breakfasted together. Then Kate went to work and Mark went wherever the mood took him, and over an evening meal she told him all about her day. He listened to her broadcasts, usually on his car radio, and always said that he had enjoyed them, that she was a bright journalist. He told her where he had been. Sometimes they ate in, often out, but Kate accepted no invitations and the only intrusion, from time to time, was the telephone.

No calls came for Mark while Kate was around, but on Thursday evening, just as they were leaving for a small out-of-town eating house, Alan phoned Kate.

She was in the hall, buttoning up her overcoat, and when he said, 'It's Alan, I'd like to talk to you,' she tasted bile and her voice was soft and savage. She said,

'Take my word for it, you would not enjoy talking to me at all.' As she cut him off she called loudly, 'Wrong number!' because in his room upstairs Mark would have heard the phone ring although he could not have heard what she was saying.

He came down almost at once, and for the rest of the evening she managed to block Alan almost entirely from her mind. She did not want to talk to him, she did not wish to see him, and she would do all that she could to avoid him. The Press Christmas Ball was going to be a problem, Alan always attended that, all the local 'celebrities' did, and by then he could be a Parliamentary candidate here. But by then Kate should be feeling stronger and Mark could still be with her. If Mark had gone and she couldn't get him back she might have to fall sick as an excuse for not turning up, but she would worry about that nearer the time.

She came out of the office around midday on Friday, on her way to an interview in another town, and she had her key in her car door when Alan said, 'Hello, Kate.'

She went rigid, although when he said, 'I've got to talk to you,' she managed to drawl,

'What's there to talk about when your letter said it all? And what the letter didn't say, Celia has.'

'I don't want you to get the wrong impression,' Alan protested incredibly. 'Because I was sincerely

in love with you. What happened between Celia and
me wasn't planned. It was like lightning striking.'

She raised her eyebrows in mock irony. 'There's
no beating the old lightning strike, is there?' And
she remembered the storm on her first night in the
tower, that great flash of lightning and thunder like
the roll of cannons. And Mark's arms around her.

Alan cleared his throat. 'You'll return my manuscript, of course?' and she nearly burst out
laughing, because that sounded like a small boy
peeping over the garden wall asking for his ball
back. Not that Alan looked like a small boy. He
looked like an embarrassed man.

'Of course,' she said. 'What would I be doing
with it? By the way, I showed it to a critic and he
said it read like a politician, pompous and long-
winded.' And she had the satisfaction of seeing him
flush angrily as she drove away.

It was a very small satisfaction. Her stomach was
churning and her head was spinning. The meeting
with Alan had left her feeling as if she had been
beaten up. She couldn't think straight. She could
hardly see straight. She was in no state to be driving
a car, nor to be doing recorded interviews this
afternoon.

But she damn well had to. She turned off the
main road into a side street where she could park
for a few minutes and sat behind the wheel forcing
herself into calmness.

She would not think of Alan. She would think
work. And Mark. She could see Mark in her mind's
eye, cynically amused; and she began to smile wryly
because he had said that about the book. She might
even tell him tonight that Alan had asked for his
masterpiece back, although on second thoughts she

was not sure she could say Alan's name without wincing, and Mark would find that suspicious.

But she could get on with the job in hand, and she arrived on time and everything there went without a hitch.

This was an item for a woman's hour programme, a diamond wedding couple who were a glowing example of sixty happily shared years. Kate found them delightful, and she was sure her listeners would. They had some good tales about the 'old days' and a canny sense of humour that made it all real and down to earth. When Kate asked, 'What would you say is the best thing about your marriage?' the woman said, 'Knowing there's always somebody there for you,' and the way they looked at each other brought a lump to Kate's throat.

That was the quote she was remembering as she walked home from the office. Knowing Mark was around had made all the difference this week. She could not imagine how she would have managed without him. She called as she opened the front door and knew at once that the house was empty. This was the first time she had arrived home first, he would be back soon, but it gave her a cold foretaste of what the future held.

She turned on lights, taking off her coat, going through the old routine as she had done countless times over the years. But for months she had believed that Alan was there for her somewhere. That had been an illusion, and so was Mark, if she was honest with herself, because he would go as surely as Alan had, if less brutally. And then, possibly for the rest of her life, she would be alone.

She went upstairs to her room and stood at the window looking down. Even the street seemed empty and she thought, loneliness is standing by the window in an empty house looking down an empty road.

Coming face to face with Alan had shaken her badly, and now she sat at her dressing-table, opening the drawer with the letters. He had said he'd loved her, that it had not all been pretence. So when did the lightning strike? Between which two letters?

She had them in dated order and she began to read from the first, trying to remember the background of each when Alan was calling her 'My own darling'.

Somewhere the loving promises became hollow, but until the very last letter they were all in the same style. Just fewer towards the end. There was no way of telling true from phoney. And how could he go on writing like this when he no longer meant a word of it?

Kate did not believe that lightning had struck. He had never been that impulsive. She had admired his analytic mind, but weighing up where his best advantage lay could also be calculating and selfish. When he realised that he could have Celia Chambers and her father's backing he had soon fallen out of love with Kate and into this grand passion for Celia.

To hell with Kate. Kate could do him no harm. And what a gullible fool he must think her, with all that guff about being sincerely in love with her but what was happening with Celia was bigger than both of them. Too right it was. Nothing came much bigger than Alan's ambitions.

Well, he could have his book back. In the morning. Delivered to his office. And that would be the end of any communication between him and Kate.

She was carrying the briefcase downstairs when there was a knock on the front door and she thought, Mark's forgotten his key. She opened the door beaming and was struck dumb. 'May I come in?' said Alan.

He walked past her, and she couldn't stop him because for a few seconds she was stunned. In the hall he looked at the briefcase and asked, 'Is it——'

She got control of her voice as angry blood rushed to her head, and she thrust the book at him, 'Your manuscript? Yes, it is. How's that for service? I can't say I was expecting you, but you certainly timed it right.'

'Thank you.' He spoke with what sounded like genuine gratitude and regret. 'I hope we can still be friends.'

She could have screamed at him, but she wanted him out of here before she lost all self-restraint and started gibbering. Then he asked, 'Do you still have my letters?'

He knew she kept them—they had joked about it. He had called her sweet and sentimental, and she felt now that she could never be either again. And why was he worrying about the letters—because the reporter in her had caught the nervous note in that casual query.

She leaned against the wall, arms folded, and said, 'Yes, I still have them.'

'May I——' he had to swallow before he could get his voice back. 'May I have them?'

'Why?' She was the investigative journalist, watching him closely. 'Who cares about a few old love letters? Not Celia, surely?'

It was fascinating reading his face, and seeing that it was not because of Celia he wanted to get his hands on his letters. So who might care? And the answer was obvious. The last thing Alan needed was publicity about the would-be-MP who believed in the old saying, promises are like piecrusts, made to be broken.

Here he was with Clifford Chambers' bimbo of a daughter, while so very recently he was swearing eternal devotion to another girl. Even the threat of a smear campaign would do for his chances of selection, he'd never get past the short list.

Kate said softly, 'When *is* the final board? Quite soon now, isn't it?'

'You wouldn't—you couldn't,' he croaked, but the letters were proof of double dealing and bad faith, and she said,

'I don't think I'll hand them over just yet.'

'How much?' It was the worst thing he could have said, fanning her fury.

'Make me an offer,' she said silkily.

'I can't believe it!' He believed he could manipulate Kate into causing no trouble, because she was so civilised, so *stupid*.

'Believe it,' she said.

'But this is blackmail.'

'Now you have it.' She grinned like an idiot. 'Go away and have a think and see what figure you come up with.'

She got him out easily. He stumbled out, and she shut the door on him, and turned to see Mark in the unlit kitchen, and that was the last straw. She wished he had not witnessed that ugly little scene, she wished it had not happened. But it had, and she was at the end of her tether.

'Don't you start!' she shrieked.

He came out into the hall. 'None of my business,' he said, and she sensed the stillness in him and wondered what it would take to shock him or shake him. 'Just one thing,' he said. 'You mentioned coming into money, great expectations, buying the tower. Was this what you had in mind?'

'Blackmail? Of course,' she said, 'I do it all the time, it's a lovely little earner. Lock up your letters while I'm about.'

Then she ran upstairs and slammed her bedroom door, blazing with fury against the whole world. If Mark thought that of her he was no friend, she would be better off without him. Tomorrow he would probably swan off anyway, but tonight she could handle no more.

She paced her room, then got into a nightshirt, and into bed, tossing and brooding until exhaustion ran through her like a drug dragging her down into sleep.

She remembered, of course, as soon as she woke. Daylight was breaking and she was cooler and calmer. She had done no more than Alan deserved—let him sweat, although she would eventually destroy or return his letters. And she could understand how it must have sounded to Mark, hearing her literally asking for money, especially after that nonsense about buying the tower. She would explain to him because that was just a misunderstanding and she did not want to lose him.

She could hear the radio, so Mark was up, and she would make her peace over a cup of coffee before she went to work.

Suddenly she jack-knifed up in bed, hurtling out and yelling as she almost fell downstairs, 'What time is it?'

'Just after seven,' he called up from the kitchen, and Kate collapsed at the bottom step with her head in her hands.

'Oh God, I'm too late!'

'For what?'

'Where's your car?' she asked.

'Up the road.'

'Mine's in the square, I forgot to move it last night.' She dragged herself into the kitchen. 'Have you ever faced a market trader who finds your car in his pitch? They took the last one apart, someone hadn't read the notice.'

Mark grinned. 'You do mean the driver?'

'Stop laughing,' she groaned. 'It's too late to do anything now. It's right in the middle, by the band-stand. They can't even push it on to the pavement, they'll have the stalls up all round it. I must get into work without being spotted.'

'You might nip down as you are and flutter your eyelashes.' She glared and he laughed, 'I must say, as a native of this town I'd have expected you to remember the local customs.'

She had never forgotten before, and she snapped, 'It's partly your fault. I lost my temper with Alan and talked a lot of rubbish, but it was you who got me really mad, believing the rubbish.'

'There you are, then—there's your excuse. The man I spent the night with sent me out of my mind.'

'Very funny!'

'Get dressed and we'll stroll along.'

Kate thought about that briefly, then said plaintively, 'Please don't crack any jokes or they could flatten my Mini.'

'I appreciate that.' Mark put on an over-solemn face that would have had her giggling any other time. 'This is a very serious matter.'

No, it was not, but it was horribly awkward and embarrassing, and left to herself she would have left it alone. She would get a parking ticket and a fine, and if the traders decided it was an obstruction and called the police she could be in more trouble because she was suddenly not sure if her MOT had run out. But there was nothing she could do about that.

She dressed in record time and said, 'I don't think it's going to make things any better. I'll just be turning up to get slagged off.'

'Don't be defeatist.' He took her arm and she had to go with him, along the road to where the market was already filling the square. Stalls were up and most of them had most of their stock on show. Early-bird customers were out, and Kate felt her mouth go dry as she approached the spot where her bright red Mini was at the centre of some red and furious faces.

The middle-aged man and woman who were Glamma-Gear were the most indignant of the lot, because the Mini was taking up half their display area, and the man's oaths rang out to a chorus of affront and sympathy. They didn't know it was Kate's car, but she looked so guilty that the woman turned on her demanding, 'Yours, is it? You ought to know better!'

They had been coming here for years. They knew who she was and where she worked. 'I'm so sorry,' she said contritely.

'Not as sorry as us,' said the man. 'Stuff piled up like pigging jumble isn't going to sell.' It was mostly lingerie, and in heaps it did lose its seductiveness.

'Why don't you make the car part of the stall?' suggested Mark. He came up with a scarlet slip. 'Red for danger,' and he fixed it like a flag on the aerial. Somebody laughed, 'It's eye-catching,' and someone else said, 'Mine's a Mini,' and looked to see where they could string some very brief briefs.

'We need some sticky tape,' said the woman, and the stall opposite produced a roll, and some coloured pens and postcards for notices, and Kate slipped away, telling herself that she didn't care what they did. They could leave the car when the market closed and she would never again forget that from eleven p.m. on Friday evening the square was out of bounds for parking.

She was in the studios all day, doing live broadcasts and making arrangements for next week, but nearly everybody who came in was laughing over Kate's sober little car being decked out in a selection ranging from see-through nightwear to winter-warm knickers. Some of the notices were raunchy, and during the afternoon the local press took pictures, coming in to ask Kate if she wanted to stand beside it.

'Get lost!' she said crossly. 'And if you show my number I'll sue you. This is strictly Glamma-Gear's baby.'

'They've written "Small but Sexy" on the boot,' said the photographer, and Kate rolled her eyes and wondered if Mark had taken any pictures himself. The whole thing had been his idea, and although it was turning into a bright little advert for Glamma-Gear she was not going near her car until it was stripped down again.

By six o'clock when Kate finished work the stalls had been dismantled and the traders had driven away. Cinema and theatregoers were moving into parking spaces in the square as she walked towards her car.

Mark and Baldy joined her, and that was nice. 'I got an offer of fifty quid for it,' he said.

'You've got to be joking!'

'You didn't see it at its best. It looked like a bordello on wheels.'

'That must have been very traumatic for it. I hope there'll be no lasting effects.'

It was shiny in the lamplight and she dug into her handbag for her keys. 'We opened it,' he said.

'You're a bundle of talents.'

'So they tell me. Talking of lasting effects,' he drew her towards the back of the car, 'apologies from the Gear family, but that seems here to stay.'

The boot read 'Small but Sexy', and Kate howled, 'I'm not driving around labelled with that!'

'So do we paint it out ourselves or do you have a friendly neighbourhood mechanic?'

During the day she had checked her MOT form in her wallet and it was due for renewal on Tuesday, so she had to get the car into a garage over the weekend. 'Anyhow,' she said, 'it isn't true. I'm not small.'

'No, you're not.' He grinned his lazy grin. 'But the rest's bang on.'

'I know that,' she said. 'I just don't advertise it.'

But half an hour at the garage took the smile off her face. Removing the slogan and retouching the paintwork was easy, but they could not issue a roadworthy certificate because her brakes were dodgy. Linings and cylinder had to be replaced and they could not guarantee getting the work done before the middle of next week.

'But I can't be without my car!' Kate wailed. 'I need it for work,' and she might have persuaded the garage owner to let her jump the queue, but Mark said,

'That's no problem, you can use mine.'

'Are you sure? I've never driven a BMW.'

'Nothing to it,' he said. 'We'll do a trial run tomorrow.'

She had never driven anyone's car but her own. Before the Mini she had had a Morris Minor. Mark's car was much flashier and more powerful, but she was sure that after a little tuition she would be able to handle it and enjoy the experience. She had all tomorrow to practise. She liked driving, she had a clean licence, and she was looking forward to him teaching her how to drive his car.

Her car had been spotted by all her friends who had gone round the market. Several phoned during the evening to share the joke and ask if she was hiring it out for commercials. 'It's in a state of shock,' she told them. 'Off the road for a day or two recuperating.'

Trish came over, smiling widely. She had bought some black satin undies threaded with red ribbon after seeing them displayed over Kate's bonnet. 'I'll be wearing them on Wednesday as one of Simon's birthday presents,' she gurgled. 'You haven't forgotten the dinner party, you did promise?'

Kate said she was looking forward to it, and Trish said, 'See you both, then.'

After Trish left Kate asked, 'Will you come with me?' and when Mark looked unenthusiastic she teased, 'You haven't met anybody since you came down here—you wouldn't be on the run?'

'Who isn't?' He was joking too. 'No, but I did tell you I'm not much of a partygoer.'

'It isn't a party.' Not like Ilse's gatherings of local society. 'Just a few friends round a table, having a meal together, but she's got her numbers balanced and there should have been eight of us.'

The invitation had been made when Kate's partner was always Alan Foster. She wondered how long it would be before he got in touch again about the letters, and her heart felt heavy, although she kept her voice light.

'It was going to be Alan and me. I don't want to let Trish down and I don't much want to go alone.'

He quirked a sardonic eyebrow. 'And if her table has an odd number the curse could fall on it?'

'Who knows? Hetty might stumble in and fill the empty chair.'

'Hetty doesn't travel well. She comes up beautifully, but she doesn't get far afield. But all right, I'll come, and we'll have their photographs ready.' Trish had wanted them for Simon's birthday, and Kate was elated.

'Where are you getting them developed?' she asked.

'I found somewhere.' There were a couple of shops in town, and she said happily,

'We'll have a lovely time, you'll see, and some delicious home cooking.' She had an almost irresistible impulse to fling her arms round him, although going over to Trish and Simon's with him was a small thing to give her this surge of delight.

As she put her hands on his shoulders and said, 'Thank you,' it was like the other time, when he found the wine glasses for her.

Very like, because he laughed and said, 'It's not that big a deal,' and took both her hands in his and still smiling held her at arm's length.

She drew her hands away and looked at them ruefully, changing the subject. 'I hope I can handle your car.'

'Of course you can. You'll take to it like a duck to water.'

'The last time I took to water I got in above my head.'

'Rely on Baldy and me,' he said. 'We'll keep you afloat.'

Sunday morning dawned fine, crisp and bright, and they drove out of town into quieter roads so that Kate could practise in comparative safety. It was a super car, she was looking forward to turning up on assignments in this, skimming down the motorways and getting wherever she was going in half her usual time.

When they stopped at a self-service station to fill up with petrol, and she was left in the car while Mark went off to pay, she peered at the dashboard trying to work out what all the dials meant. There was a small Sunday morning queue in the station, confectionery, cigarettes and newspapers were also on sale here, and she opened the glove compartment and gasped as a letter literally fell into her hands.

She didn't think she had been prying, but when she looked for Mark he was still behind several other customers and she glanced down at the folded letter and read, 'Dearest, I'm lying here in my lonely little bed remembering our incredible weekend.'

She shoved it back as hastily as if it was dusted with poison, then took it out again very carefully to read the signature, 'Love you, *love* you, Denise.'

One thing was sure. The incredible weekend had not been spent doing the tourist sights, and jealousy lanced her like a thin sharp knife. She *had* been prying, starting to read and then looking for a signature, and it was no surprise, because Mark was the last man you would mistake for a monk, and although he had been with Kate in a fashion for over three weeks that didn't mean he was not in touch with Denise.

So who was she? What did she look like? Had there been a quarrel? Did that explain his black mood on the night of the storm, and the casual non-committal way he had taken up with Kate?

The stab of jealousy had gone deep, and she watched him come out of the building and walk across the forecourt with that panther-like stride and knew she had wanted him for what seemed a long time. She could hear her heartbeats, fast and deafening, as he came nearer, and when he slipped into the driving seat beside her her fingers clasped and tightened.

She had thought he would be a dangerously accomplished lover, so it would be safe and sensible to keep things between them the way they were for as long as she could. But the letter had stirred her imagination so that she was picturing that weekend in slow erotic motion.

She saw his hands on the wheel and felt them stroking her, while the slight controlled movements of his body seemed to reach her skin and set fire to her blood. It was lust pure and simple, but violent enough to play havoc with her senses.

Out of the garage forecourt Mark drew up beside the road and adjusted the driving seat. 'Move over,' he said, and came round to her side of the car.

Kate squirmed herself behind the wheel. It would have been better if she had had some time to get over the shock of finding out how much she wanted this man. When he touched her now the little thrills she had felt before were turning into mega-volts, so that she almost shot out of her seat and had to bite her lip to listen to the instructions he was giving her.

She wanted to say, 'I've got the shakes,' but of course she couldn't, so she turned on the ignition and started the car, moving slowly away. When she wobbled over the controls he put a steadying hand on hers and she nearly jerked them into the ditch.

He grabbed the wheel and straightened the car, and looked hard at her, and now there was more reason than ever why she couldn't meet his eyes. She sat back, letting him lean over and guide the car to a halt.

'So much for the first lesson,' she said shakily.

'What *is* the matter?'

She couldn't pretend she was not tense when she was twitching with nerves, but she tried to laugh. 'I'll be all right once I get the hang of it.'

'It's the bit in between that I'm worrying about,' Mark said drily. 'I'm not sure I want you driving my car before you get the hang.' She had just been reading an intimate letter, and under the disturbing directness of his gaze her face flamed, making her look hot and bothered. 'Tell you what,' he said, taking pity on her, 'I'll chauffeur you. I'm going nowhere in particular for the next few days, so I'll drive you around.'

'That would be—very helpful,' she stammered.

'Right, then. Let's move over again.'

He was out of his door and she got out of hers as Baldy watched them both with mild interest. The driver's seat was readjusted and by now Kate was calming down. But she could never again fool herself that she was not eager to make love with Mark. Aching for him, longing to lose herself in his arms without thinking about tomorrow or next month or anybody or anything else.

This hunger must have been building up in her. She had repressed it and she would control it, but, although Mark didn't know, for Kate their relationship had changed.

When he said, 'I thought you were a natural driver,' she babbled,

'It's a powerful car. Too much engine power seems to make me nervous.' She pulled a woeful face. 'But thanks for the taxi offer, that would suit me perfectly.'

'It would suit me too.' He touched her hair gently, tucking a lock, that had fallen over her eyes, behind her ear, and that was enough to make her senses reel.

She thought, I am not falling in love. I am never going to fall in love again. But if you and Denise should have quarrelled, and it should be over between you, that would make me very happy...

CHAPTER SIX

NOTHING was seen to have changed. Mark and Kate
spent Sunday out together, and although Kate was
consumed with curiosity over the letter she could
hardly say, 'By the way, I told you to lock up your
letters, so who's Denise?'

Very briefly she had the crazy idea of sniffing
and enquiring, 'Do you have a tissue?' opening the
glove compartment and making the letter fall out,
and waiting for his reaction. But she didn't think
she would get one. She thought Mark would re-
place the letter and tell her nothing. If she asked
bluntly, 'Who's it from?' she would be asking for
a brush-off, because he was not a man to tolerate
trespassers beyond the bounds he set himself.

Three weeks together and sometimes she thought
she knew him well, but most times she was aware
of a barrier she had never breached. Beyond that
she might not even like him, but the chemistry was
fierce and she was not going to fight it. If she and
Mark became lovers she could pay for it later, but
if she let him go without taking all the joy that their
closeness offered her regret would be sure and bitter.

They had always been near a sexual relationship.
It had always seemed up to Kate to make the small
move from friends to lovers, still smiling maybe,
still fooling, with no promises for the future.

Well, she would settle for that. What use were
promises? Alan's letters had been full of them. She
wanted Mark and she thought he wanted her. Not

enough to pressure her, but surely he would take what she offered, and that was enough to fill her with an excited shyness like a young girl at the start of her first affair.

She went to her own room that night. If he had kissed her when he said goodnight she could have pressed closer, but he didn't. He said, 'Sleep well, Katy,' and she couldn't get out the words, 'Will you sleep with me?'

She had to be less sophisticated than she thought, because shyness was inhibiting her. But she fell asleep dreaming herself into his arms, and woke next morning knowing that the chill of daylight was not cooling the fever in her blood.

So, she was no different from the other women who simpered when they met him. She fancied Mark Brandon. Her advantage was that for a little while they would be living together, and sleeping together before long.

By the end of this week, she promised herself, we will be lovers. If it didn't happen soon she would make it happen. She would only have to fling her arms around him, giving the caress, offering the rest; and she could do that naturally enough saying thank-you for something.

On Wednesday, after Trish's dinner party, it could be for the photographs, because she was almost sure they would be good and Trish and Simon would be pleased with them. It would be an enjoyable evening and Kate would be looking her best. Mark had called her sensational when she dressed up for Ilse's party, only this time when she stepped out of her sequinned sheath dress she would be more sensational than ever. Simon's thirty-something birthday would be a night to remember, not only for Simon and Trish in her flirty scarlet ribbons.

Kate was glad she had failed the test on his car, because on Monday Mark was ferrying her around. A year ago gales and heavy snowfalls had swept across the area, bringing down power lines, immobilising traffic. Homes, schools and factories had been blacked out, motorists trapped in iced-up convoys. There was no sign of snow yet, but Kate was following last year's reports for a programme, *When the Lights Went Out*.

The Midlands usually escaped the worst of the winter weather, the blizzards had been early and freakish, and most of those who had been badly hit reminisced now as if they had rather enjoyed themselves.

'It was like the Blitz,' said one old lady happily. 'Everybody helping everybody else. Those who'd got open fires did the cooking. The young ones had barbecues in the snow. Oil lamps and candles, and we wrapped ourselves up against the cold.'

A year ago Kate had talked to a mother of four young children, in an isolated house without power or water, who had been on the verge of a nervous breakdown but who now spoke of it as though it had brought out her pioneering spirit.

Nobody wanted a recurrence, but as it was eight years since the previous freeze-up they felt fairly safe and, looking back, it had been an adventure.

Mark kept out of the way while Kate was interviewing, walking around with Baldy, or staying in the car, and each time she came out to join him and move on, her spirits rose. As she settled into the passenger seat, with a map and the next address on her knee, she said, 'I could get used to this. What are your terms for long-term taxi service?'

He smiled across at her. 'Too much. Long-term I'm a bad risk.'

That was probably a warning, but she talked nonsense back. 'I couldn't afford you at any price, and it's more fun being ferried for free.'

She wouldn't worry about the long term. She would just enjoy today and look forward to tomorrow, and Wednesday was the day and the night after that.

She said, 'If we'd been driving down this road a year ago today we'd have been heading into the blizzard, and just over the hill a lorry would have jack-knifed and we'd soon be in a queue of traffic stretching for miles and stuck for three days and two nights. Villagers brought them food out, but most of them dossed down in their cars.'

'We wouldn't have frozen with Baldy around,' said Mark, and she thought, I wouldn't have minded too much. Huddled that close for that long would have had some marvellous moments.

Next day Kate was sent out in the radio car so she had no transport problem, and on Wednesday she got her Mini back with its repaired brakes and its roadworthy chit.

She came home to Mark on Wednesday, keeping her fingers crossed until she saw his car parked in the square. She was later than usual. Her schedule was flexible, but tonight she had wanted plenty of time to get ready for the party and she almost ran up the road.

He was watching a news programme on TV, sitting with the dog at his feet, and she called from the hall, 'You haven't forgotten about tonight?' She had mentioned it again during breakfast, of course he hadn't forgotten, but there was a few seconds' silence, while she hoped he was not having second thoughts, before he said,

'I'll be with you. There's no rush, is there?'

Just over an hour, and Trish wouldn't mind if they turned up as they were. But this was the night that Kate planned her seduction scene, and sweater and skirt and hair blown all ways were not going to give her the confidence she needed to feel irresistible.

She said, 'I'll call down when I'm through with the bathroom. You don't have to pretty up, but I shall.'

She chose the black sequinned dress again. She felt good in it and Mark had liked it. They made a good pair, he had said last time she wore it, and she had smiled, but tonight she might say that without smiling because this time she was in earnest.

They were good together in all the superficial ways. She had never known anyone she got along with so easily. But deeper, under the skin, she was sure it would be incredible. Just thinking of love-making with Mark nearly had her swooning. She closed her eyes and swayed, wrapping her arms around herself.

Then she sat down at her dressing-table and although she had only just finished fixing her hair and her face, she stared hard at her reflection, checking for flaws. She thought she was satisfied. She had to be, because this was the best she could do and less than a month ago she had believed she was beautiful.

The letters that told her so were still in the drawer. Some time she would have to take them out and get rid of them. Not hand them back. That could mean another scene, maybe seeing Alan again. There was no open fire in the house so she couldn't burn them, but she could tear them up and dustbin them. She didn't want to read them again, she didn't even want to touch them because the pain was still there, and maybe this craving she had for Mark was only to show herself she was still desirable.

He tapped on her door and she called, 'Come in,' turning to smile, then gasping, 'Wow!'

He was wearing dark grey trousers and jacket, superbly cut; grey shirt and grey silk tie. A complete change from his usual casual clothes, he now looked distinguished enough to chair any company board meeting.

She croaked, 'You never brought that in the duffle bag?'

'I shopped. I didn't realise I was staying so long.'

She rushed to remind him, 'I stayed a fortnight in your tower; you haven't had two weeks yet. You're very welcome to stay on.'

'Thank you,' he said, 'but that wouldn't be very practical,' and before she could argue, 'If you're ready I've something to show you.'

She followed him downstairs and she saw what it was. A large envelope and photographs were on the low table in front of the settee. She sat down beside him and he handed her a black and white five-by-eight-inch shot of a church corbel, a fat smiling face with a monk's fringe of hair. It was weathered and worn, but there was a slyness about it that made Kate say, 'I wouldn't trust him far. Where is he?'

'Your local, St Giles.'

The church dated from the Middle Ages and every archway had its supporting sculpture. Kate must have seen them all, but she had never looked this closely. It was as though the photographer had caught him unawares, and she asked, 'Does he always look like this?'

'Only when the north light gets him,' said Mark.

The photographs he had taken around the area: buildings, streets, vistas, all had something original and striking about them. When people were included they were so alive that she could almost see them breathing. One, taken in the market last Saturday, had Mrs Gear Blu-Tacking a pair of panties to the windscreen of the Mini with a malevolent grin, and Kate burst out laughing because it was a vivid warning to parkers not to leave their cars around on market mornings.

'They're brilliant,' she said.

'Thank you.'

As she turned to the pictures of the twins she was lost for words. Every one seemed a masterpiece. In each Mark had caught their impish spirits. In one they were glaring at each other, in another their smiles showed the bond between them. The rapport included Baldy, and that was a beautiful study, the wide-eyed children and the dog's great dark head.

She said at last, 'Trish will be beside herself when she sees these. They're superb, terrific.'

'Thank you again.'

'You're good, aren't you?'

'Yes.' Anything else would have been the falsest of modesty, and the pictures of her over the Chinese takeaway showed again how skilled he was. She was beautiful here, a model girl for the glossies, and she asked,

'May I keep them? I'm never going to get a better ego-trip than these.'

She had told him that the last one would not be up to much, and he had said, 'We'll see.' 'Look at me, Kate,' he had said, and as always she had found it hard to do that. Her lids had drooped over her eyes and her mouth had curved in a tight-lipped smile.

It was not like the others, which were shining and gorgeous. The candlelight seemed to play more part, emphasising shadows. 'Katy by Candlelight,' he said. 'The Mona Lisa smile, a girl with secrets. What are your secrets, Katy?'

Her light laugh sounded nervous. 'I don't have secrets, I'm a simple soul. How about you?'

'What you see is what you get,' he said cheerfully, which was no answer at all, although what she was seeing was pretty impressive. 'Shall we go?' he said.

'How about Baldy?'

'He'll be all right.'

'He knows you'll be back?'

'That's right.'

This time she said it aloud, 'Lucky for him,' then she put the twins' photographs into the envelope and picked up the package that was aftershave for Simon.

She couldn't get over the way Mark looked. That was an expensive suit, it had to change his image. He was as relaxed as ever, but Kate was feeling very slightly less comfortable with him.

Clothes shouldn't be doing that, it had to be the stunning photographs. She had been unprepared for them being so good it was scary. And she had been right about those piercing eyes, they could see

what anyone else might miss, so it was as well she
had instinctively shied away from eye contact.

But when he put a hand under her elbow, as they
crossed the road, she was suddenly hollow with
longing. That isn't changing, she thought wryly, I
still want him like crazy.

The lights were all on in Trish's windows and the
door opened before Kate could get her finger off
the bell. Simon's birthday guests were old friends:
Trish's sister and her husband, the science master
from the Poly where Simon taught maths and the
girl he was marrying some time. And Kate.

Mark was the newcomer. They had all accepted
Alan Foster and Kate Kershaw as a steady item.
Now Kate was living with another man who had
kept a very low profile since she came back from
holiday with him.

The men were interested. Foster was up-and-
coming in politics, well off and a catch. They wondered vaguely who Kate was replacing him with.

But the two women were agog. Trish had described Mark to them as 'A really hot number, the
sort who sends shivers down your spine just looking
at you.' As Kate and Mark stepped into the house
and Trish said, 'I was just coming over to fetch
you,' Emma her sister, and Liz, crowded into the
hall behind her.

Trish and Simon's house was the same design as
Kate's but three-bedroomed with a wider hall, and
the main room, seen through the open door, about
twice the size of Kate's living-room. They all had
pre-dinner glasses in their hands, and Trish said,
'This is Mark,' with a glance at the girls that said,
Didn't I tell you?

Kate was telling herself, this is what I wanted. My friends meeting Mark and being impressed. She stood back during the handshakes and the initial hellos while they were all sizing him up, and it couldn't have been better. The men were obviously deciding he was someone to be reckoned with, and Liz and Emma were looking as though the party had suddenly taken off.

Both girls were spoken for and very content with their lot, but Trish had been right, Kate's new man did put an edge on things. Into a pleasant predictable evening he brought a thrilling whiff of danger. He was so lean and dark, and taller than the other men. He *looked* dangerous, and there was no one in the room who was not intrigued.

Kate watched the little crowd around him. Nobody would be pitying her tonight because Alan was not with her, but it was not unalloyed triumph. Everyone thought Mark was her lover, and she would have liked to put a hand on his arm and face them with a 'he's mine' smile. There was nothing to stop her doing that, but it would have been pretence, because she had no claim on him at all, and she was suddenly unsure if getting herself into his bed tonight might cost her too dearly in the end.

She was feeling possessive right now while all was platonic between them. After she had made love with him she might find out what jealousy really meant.

'All right, Kate?' Trish asked beside her, and Kate smiled brightly.

'Sure I am. Only it was rather a rush, I was working late. Happy birthday, Simon.' She presented him with the aftershave, which he unwrapped and enthused over.

'How did you know it's my favourite?'

She had asked Trish, but she laughed, 'Oh, I've got a nose for a good aftershave. And here's what Trish ordered for an extra present.' She gave Trish the envelope.

'The photographs?' Trish sounded apprehensive. 'You should have seen the last lot,' she said to Mark. 'But thank you very much.'

She took them out, staring at the first, then the second, then saying huskily, 'Oh, my! Oh, they're lovely—oh, darling, *look*!' and handing them to Simon.

Of course they all knew the twins—who were with grandparents tonight—and they all thought the pictures were brilliant. Kate was touched to see Trish's eyes misting with motherly pride as she gazed fondly at the one with the dog. 'I don't know which is my favourite, they're all super. I must settle up before you go.'

Mark shrugged payment away. 'Happy birthday,' he said, and Trish blushed.

'Oh, we couldn't! I mean, they're beautiful, but I wasn't angling for a freebie when I asked Kate——'

'Thanks very much,' said Simon promptly.

'Do you do weddings?' asked Liz. 'Not that we've fixed a date yet, but when we do can we get in touch?'

Mark said, 'Do that,' and Kate was the only one who knew by the quirk of his mouth that this was amusing him. Of course he would be long gone before Liz and Andrew named the day, but that didn't make Kate feel like smiling.

The meal was delicious, starting with chilled cucumber soup, then lasagne and a rather spectacular salad for the vegetarians, Emma and Fergus, and *tournedos* with mushrooms for the rest.

As Kate had expected, Mark was a great asset to this party. He was funny and relaxed and apparently outgoing. It was Kate who told them about the Martello tower, but then he answered all their questions about it, and in a smaller way Trish and Simon had done the same kind of thing.

Just after they got married, a great-aunt of Simon's had left him a tumbledown cottage in Yorkshire which they had renovated, using for holidays ever since.

Kate had been there and she would probably go again, but the tower was up for sale. It might have been her one and only visit, and she said wistfully, 'I couldn't bear to sell the tower if it was mine. It's a fantastic old place, full of history and atmosphere.'

'Is it haunted?' Emma leaned forward in her chair, she loved ghost stories, and Kate remembered what Mark had said about photographing ghosts.

'Is it?' she asked.

'They do say,' said Mark solemnly, 'that a dark shapeless figure has been seen sitting at a table, and, nearby, feet without legs.'

'What is it?' gasped Emma. 'What was it all about?'

'Who knows?' said Mark, and Kate wondered if her coat and shoes were still where she had left them, and decided it would be a shame to laugh and spoil it for Emma.

In the kitchen, between the main course and the raspberry meringue pie and praline icecream, the

girls cornered Kate to find out 'How long is he
staying?'

'He's self-employed,' she said blandly. 'He works
from the shop during the summer and freelances
during the winter. He can stay as long as he likes.'

Mark had said that would not be practical, but
it could be. 'Lodging with you?' Liz probed archly,
and Kate smiled what Mark had called her Mona
Lisa smile. 'He more than pays his way, but I
wouldn't call him a lodger.'

That satisfied them. They carried in the dishes
and settled down again, convinced that Kate had
struck lucky and come up with a super replacement
for Alan.

No one was driving home. Andrew had booked
a midnight taxi, Emma and Fergus lived in walking
distance. So the wine flowed and the party fizzed,
and when they sat with Gaelic coffees it was a
mellow gathering of friends.

Trish smiled across at Kate, because this had been
one of her best dinner parties ever and Kate's new
man was proving a star turn. You can bring him
any time, Trish was signalling, he's a charmer.

Kate thought so too. Simon was holding forth
now, telling a rambling tale about a pompous guest
lecturer at the college who had forgotten his notes
and given completely the wrong speech. Mark was
the only one who had not heard this before. Andrew
had been there and helped the story along, and it
was funny, and Mark was laughing as he listened.

Kate looked at him, thinking how pleasant it all
was, glad that Mark was enjoying his evening. And
he *was*, no doubt about that, but not quite as the
others were. They were all slightly lit and he was
cold sober.

She blinked, because he had drunk as much as she had and he was being very good company. Everybody liked him. They thought they were accepting him and including him. Only Kate knew that he was a smiling outsider, taking no real part in all this mateyness.

She also knew that he was the toughest man here and she was probably no closer to him than anyone else round this table, and her gaiety was doused like cold water on a little flame.

Then as Simon's story ended Fergus picked up a bottle of the good red wine that was only half empty. 'We can't be leaving this.' He looked at the glasses. 'Trish?' She nodded and he poured for her. 'Kate? Alan?'

'No, thank you,' said Kate, and Fergus jumped, sprinkling wine liberally over the pretty pink cloth as his wife kicked him under the table.

That caused a small furore. Trish was no fusser, but it was her favourite tablecloth and red wine was notorious for staining. So the cloth was whipped off and given first aid in the kitchen, and by the time that was done the taxi had arrived. Andrew and Liz gave Emma and Fergus a lift, and Kate and Mark were left, the last of the guests.

Trish drew Kate aside to whisper, 'Do you think he noticed, Fergus calling him Alan?'

Kate shrugged. 'There's not much gets past that one, he doesn't miss a thing.'

'I hope he's not the jealous kind,' Trish muttered.

'It doesn't matter,' said Kate. 'He wouldn't mind.'

Nor would he mind, and that did matter, to Kate.

'We were thinking before you came,' said Trish, raising her voice to reach the men. 'My mum had

the twins tonight, so Simon's mother's having them
for us over the weekend and we're going up to the
cottage. Why don't you two come on Saturday and
stay till Sunday or Monday morning? There's a
spare room and a bed going spare.'

Kate said quickly, 'May we let you know?' Then
she thanked Trish for a lovely evening and a lovely
meal, and Mark thanked them both, and Trish and
Simon looked at each other as they watched Kate
and Mark crossing the road.

'She didn't waste much time, did she?' said
Simon. 'And here you were worrying that Alan
Foster was going to break her.'

'Well, he didn't, did he?' said Trish. 'So how
about this one?'

'I wouldn't like to get on the wrong side of him,'
said Simon.

The door on the other side of the road opened.
Kate and the tall dark man were silhouetted in light
as Trish closed her own door, happy for Kate but
still just a little concerned for her too.

Baldy threw himself at Mark with frantic enthusiasm, then welcomed Kate as an afterthought.
'It was a good evening, wasn't it?' she said. 'You
liked them, didn't you?'

'It was, and I did.' He seemed to mean that, and
now they were alone and going upstairs in the next
few minutes. Baldy needed a short walk. Mark let
him out through the back door, beyond the patio,
and Kate sat on the bottom of the stairs and waited.

She did want to sleep with Mark. It had been
easy enough to plan how she would get round to
it, but how did she know how he would react to an
outright offer? He might not fancy a change in their

relationship. Sex could be a tie of sorts. He might feel it might hold him, and he might not want that.

Now the moment had come and she was nervous. Still basically insecure, she was half prepared for another rejection, and when she heard him in the house she took a deep gulp of air and got shakily to her feet.

Standing there, she breathed deeply again and started, 'We could make a night of it.'

He steadied her, smiling down at her. 'You're working tomorrow, you need your sleep. And I never take advantage of a lady in her cups.'

He was making a joke of a brush-off, and so must she. 'That is a very priggish attitude,' she said.

'Not the first time, anyway.' It could have been worse. Then he asked, 'Are we going away at the weekend?'

'If you like.'

'I'd like that.'

'Me too,' she said, and went ahead upstairs, undressing and cleaning off her make-up and getting into bed, glowing with delight. This was not a rejection. This was a commitment, for a little while.

She lay, waiting for sleep, her flushed cheek against the cool cotton of the pillow, and her last drowsy thought was that the way her feelings for Mark were going was almost like falling in love.

Kate's bright idea about the photographs came as she was walking to work next morning. If Mark had been with her she would have discussed it with him, of course, but he was still back at the house, and anyway she could see no reason why he should object.

She was taking the pictures into the studios to show her workmates, and she passed the local newspaper office—with its window of current affairs, snapped mostly by staff photographers—when she saw her Mini. It made a good picture as a lingerie display, but the one of Mrs Gear, sticking up panties and grinning like a witch, had the master touch.

Mark was freelancing, and that was one photograph that should definitely have sold. It still could, and if Kate found an outlet here for his work he might be more likely to stay, certainly to keep in touch.

She knew all the staff on the *Despatch* and she got straight in to see the art editor, who looked up from his desk to say, 'Hello, Kate, what can we do for you?'

'I've brought you some pictures.' This was a weekly, coming out on Saturday, so there was time to catch the next edition, and she took it out of her briefcase and handed it over.

Lawson Trout was well named—rather fishlike, with pale protuberant eyes, and now his mouth opened and closed. Then he chuckled, 'Not bad at all.'

'These are local scenes.' She showed him the rest, only holding her own pictures back.

His eyebrows went up and down as he gave several grunts of approval. Then he said,

'You didn't take them?'

'Not me, no. I've got a friend staying with me, a freelance. Are you interested?'

'Could be.' He wasn't fooling her. She knew she would have to prise his plump fingers off them. 'Ask him to come in and have a chat.'

'Right.' She had no time to start talking terms, that would be up to Mark. She would ring home and tell him that the local Press was drooling over his work and if he strolled into the office in the square he would probably make a killing.

But it was a little while before she could make the call, and then her home number rang unanswered. And during the day, she tried several times, but when she finished work Mark's car was parked, so he was back from wherever he had been.

The pictures of Kate had been oohed and aahed over by the women who worked with her. She could have got commissions for portraits there, but of course she could promise nothing. She would tell Mark and he would decide what he wanted to do, and the newspaper should be a good market, because the *Despatch* covered the county and beyond and was a classy little number.

Whatever came of it all she hoped she had done the groundwork for Mark Brandon to start operating in her area, and she let herself into the house wondering what news to give him first.

Baldy came into the hall from the living-room as Mark came out of the kitchen. 'Had a good day?' asked Kate.

'Yes. You?'

'Busy.' She hung her coat in the closet. 'I showed all of them your pictures.' A shuttered look came over his face. 'Everybody raved about them,' she said happily. 'All the girls at work want you to photograph them, and the art editor on the *Despatch* can't wait to meet you.'

When he looked at her now she recognised the man who had turned on her that first night, when she had intruded on him during the storm. A fierce impatience reached her so that she moved back a step, almost as if she was dodging a blow.

His voice was toneless. 'And who asked you to tout my stuff around?'

'Nobody.' He knew that, but what harm had she done? 'I'm sorry, I thought——'

'Half the trouble in the world,' he said grimly, 'is caused by idiots who are sorry but they thought——' and how could she have imagined there was friendship between them when he was so contemptuous of any help she could give him?

She thought she was doing him a favour and she had expected him to be pleased. Talk about male arrogance! Calling her an idiot, rounding on her as if he had caught her going through his private papers!

The letter signed Denise came into her mind and she thought, You're welcome to him. He's a Jekyll and Hyde.

She said, trying for cutting dignity, 'Forget the whole thing. I promised nobody anything.' She might have gone on to say that this was the last time she would interfere in anything remotely concerning him. And if he was clearing off tomorrow she would not give anybody his address. In fact she would guarantee to forget it.

But a stupid lump was rising in her throat, and she went up the stairs two at a time, because the rebuff had been such a shock. It was worse because she surely knew why. Mark did not want her help, nor anybody's, from the sound of it. But that was not all. He had seen through her scheme to keep him here and he was having none of it. Last night she had been scared of rejection, but the thought of the weekend at the cottage, sharing a room, sharing a bed, had kept her happy and hopeful.

Which was fine by him, until she came home tonight with long-term plans. He had warned her he was a bad long-term risk, but she had gone right ahead, and now he was making it brutally clear that his future would not be including her.

She was shaking with disappointment and hurt and anger. A crazy cocktail that made her head swim so that her knees buckled and she flopped down on the stool in front of her dressing-table and gripped the table edge to steady herself.

When she was calmer she would go downstairs, because this was her house and in it she kept out of nobody's way. He might apologise, he had been appallingly boorish, and although he was accepting no help from her he might have cooled down.

If he had she would say 'Forget it,' although neither of them would. There was no question of that weekend together now. No question of anything. He could hardly have reacted more savagely if he had knocked her down, and she stared at her white-faced reflection.

No wonder she looked sorry for herself! Three times unlucky, she had to be a born loser. And a fool, because she had been well on the way to falling in love with Mark. She had learned nothing from the pain Alan had caused her so recently, although she only had to open that drawer and read a few letters to remind herself she was a loser and that she should stop being a fool.

She pulled a drawer open now, took the top letter out of its envelope and began to tear it up, letting the pieces fall down into the drawer. After a few minutes it was almost relaxing, like playing with worry beads, and she worked rhythmically, scattering a coarse confetti over the remaining letters.

When she heard the knock on the front door she hesitated, before she closed the drawer and got up to answer it. Whoever was there she would plead a headache, and the next few days would explain why, when Mark Brandon left town.

But the door below was already open. Mark had answered it, and from the top of the stairs Kate heard a male voice bellowing, 'Well, I'll be beggared—Tad Brand! What's all this, then, Kate's fun and games?'

'Something like that.' Mark . . . Tad . . . whoever, was laughing, and Lawson Trout reeled in, still wheezing.

'Bloody good pictures. Can't afford your prices, though. Pity!'

'Have them on the house,' said Mark, who was not Mark to the people who knew him, and Kate stepped back into her room, sitting down again, this time on the bed.

Her mind was clearing wonderfully. Suddenly everything made sense. He was no undiscovered genius. He was an international name. Of all the photographers in the shop the beauty queen was probably the only one he had taken himself, and no wonder he blew when Kate had shown his work around town. The last thing he wanted was publicity.

Trish would be thrilled, but hardly surprised, to hear she had a free set of some very exclusive and expensive photography, and Kate was calming down rapidly, to the stage where all the heat seemed to have gone out of her.

But he should have told her. All right, he wanted no fuss, no reminding of the killing fields, the madness and mayhem, that made up his working life; and if she had known she would have never tried to drag him to parties, much less offered his photographs to a pressman who had met him before.

He should have trusted her. If he had not told her at the beginning there had been countless times since when he could have said who he was, and she would have recognised the name. And if he had wanted to stay incognito she would have understood why.

He had just called her an idiot, but he was the one who had made her act idiotically, keeping her in the dark when there was no reason for it, except that it must have been amusing him.

She heard the front door close, so Lawson Trout had not stayed long. He would be chuckling all the way back to the office, over the pictures he'd got for nothing, and the joke of Kate not knowing who she'd got staying in her home.

She came downstairs demanding resentfully, 'Why didn't you tell me you're a top pro?' She followed him into the living-room. 'I feel such a *fool*!' and her voice rose so shrilly that he drawled,

'Aren't you overreacting? I'm not a serial killer. I'm a bloke with a camera who's got about. What's the problem?'

She could hardly believe her ears. 'The problem is that I didn't *know*. I bring you here and it looks as if we're living together!' His eyebrows rose. He wouldn't care what it looked like, but she did, and she spaced her words for emphasis. 'And I don't even know your name.'

'Thaddeus Mark Brandon.'

'Tad Brand. Does anyone call you Mark?'

'No.'

'Then why did you let me?'

'You seemed to fancy it, and my surname is Brandon. There was a time when my father disapproved of my kind of work.'

'There's a fascinating thing, I'm learning something new about you all the time. Well, the joke's on me again,' Kate said bitterly.

'What joke?'

She stood with her head thrown back and her arms folded. 'First there's Philip, who takes a slow boat to Australia the day before the wedding.'

'Why Australia?' he asked as if that had any bearing on anything, but she answered automatically,

'His mother packed him off, they'd got relations there. Then Alan, who was two-timing me, only I was too thick to see it. And now my very good mate the well-known photographer, who must be laughing his socks off because——' now she was almost shouting '—I didn't even know his bloody name!'

'So what?' He sounded as if she was throwing a childish tantrum. 'Why should it matter what name I work under? What difference does it make?'

'The difference that they're all going to be sorry for me being made a fool of again!'

He still looked as if she was talking nonsense, and so she was to someone like him. 'You don't understand what that means, do you?' she cried. 'People pitying you.'

She went to the patio window, not seeing anything in the darkness outside but because it was easier to talk with her back to him. 'Well, I'm an expert in it, right from when my father walked out on us and my mother soaked up sympathy like a sponge. She loved it. She was always sighing and looking sad, and I used to cringe and hate it. I was seventeen when she died, and after Philip jilted me everyone went straight back to calling me poor Kate. As if it was my name. Nobody but you ever did call me Katy, but everybody called me poor Kate.

'Of course they kept telling me it wasn't my fault Philip had gone, just as they did when my father went. But there's a kind of gloating behind pity after a while, that it isn't happening to them. That's when you know they're beginning to wonder if it is your fault.'

He was standing just behind her. She could see his reflection in the dark glass. 'And it was going to start up again when I lost Alan,' she said, quietly now, 'only you came back with me, so it didn't.'

In the silence following that he said, 'You asked me back here so that your friends shouldn't feel sorry for you?'

She might have denied it if she had not been too drained for anything but a muttered 'Yes.'

'You do have secrets, Kate,' and when she turned he raised an eyebrow. 'Working, was it?'

'Of course.'

'Glad to be of service,' he said drily as hot colour flared on her cheekbones.

'I talk too much.' She felt wretched. 'I sound so sorry for myself.'

'Yes, you do.' She had not expected him to understand, but then he said quite gently, 'You're

not the only walking wounded,' and she stared at
him as the words sank in, knowing them for the
truth. Coming from a man who had seen the world
at its worst it made her own troubles seem less than
terrible, and she felt bitterness slipping away, releasing her from the past.

At the same time the future stretched ahead, flat
and dreary. She might have had a chance with Mark
Brandon who had a small studio and was unknown
outside his home town.

With Tad Brand there was no hope at all. The
competition would be immeasurably beyond anything she had to offer.

CHAPTER SEVEN

'WHAT do I call you, Mark or Tad?' Kate wondered.

'I'll answer to either.'

After a moment she said, 'I think I'll stay with Mark,' and he said,

'And I shall stay with Katy.'

The name, he meant, not the girl, but it was a small sharing, names that nobody else used, and she smiled, 'Not poor Kate?'

'Certainly not.' He sat down in his usual chair and she knew that for her that would be Mark's chair long after he had gone. 'Do you want to tell us about it?'

The dog's bright eyes and the man's hooded eyes were on her as she sat on the sofa opposite, wrapping her arms around herself, keeping her voice steady. 'There's not much more to tell. I went on holiday because I had time off and he was going to America on business.'

She had gone to the tower and surely that was meant, because finding Mark had had so much more impact on her than losing Alan. 'It wasn't to give us time to think about each other,' she said. 'He was already having an affair with another girl, but I hadn't a clue about that until I phoned back here and a friend told me.'

She shook her head at her own stupidity. 'I was actually expecting him to announce our engagement! There's this emerald and seed pearl ring

155

that belonged to his grandmother that I tried on. In secret, but I thought it was a rehearsal.' She went on shaking her head, slowly. 'Pearls are for tears, aren't they, and aren't emeralds unlucky?'

'I wouldn't know.'

'Well, they should be. And that's it. Jilted again.' She pulled a wry face. 'Silly sort of word. It sounds old-fashioned, Victorian, but there's still plenty of it going on.'

'Who is he?' he asked.

'Alan?' Of course. 'Well, his name's Alan Foster. You saw his photograph, the half-a-Mars-bar man. The family business is engineering, quite a big concern, and as I told you he's into politics. He could be our local candidate for Parliament next time round. He's got it all planned, he's very ambitious.'

'Was that his attraction for you?' Mark was lounging in the deep chair, looking and sounding lazy, drawing the confidences out of her so that she admitted,

'Probably. I was so insecure after my father and Philip that Alan seemed like a rock.' She remembered the rocks of the causeway and the waves sweeping over her and Mark getting her ashore . . .

'Was there anyone else for you?' he was asking.

'No.' But she had not met Mark then. Her sigh was because Mark hardly wanted her at all, not because Alan had found another lover.

'So who did he exchange you for?' he asked bluntly, and that wiped the wistfulness from her face.

'A better bet—a real asset. Her father has plenty of local political pull. His name's Clifford Chambers.'

'Ah!'

'You've heard of him?'

'I've met him.' Three long seconds ticked in her head before he added, 'And Celia.'

She gulped, 'What—did you think of her?'

'Very pretty.'

Before she could stop herself she had snapped, 'If you like Barbie dolls.'

'Yes,' he went along with that. Celia Chambers, blonde and pertly perfect, did have a doll-like quality; and suddenly Kate felt so hostile towards her that it was all she could do not to say, 'She's a spoiled little dimwit.' Instead she said, 'Celia was at that party for your first day here. If we'd gone along she'd have recognised you.'

Somebody was bound to eventually, but she was glad it had not happened right away. She had enjoyed their time alone together. Now she would be sharing him, and she tried to be professional. 'May I interview you?' she asked. 'Radio Danilo can always use a visiting celebrity.'

'No, you may not.'

'Off the record, then.' She had told him all manner of things. Not the secret deep in her heart, that she loved him, but she had talked about everything else. 'You owe me some answers.'

'Such as?'

'How about that shop, with your father's name over it? Who does run it?'

'Bill Latymer, he worked for my father. Now he and his wife live where we used to live, over the shop. I still have a room there.'

'You live in the tower?'

'Some of the time, when I'm in England. Mostly it's out of suitcases.' He grinned reminiscently.

'When I first started I lived with the travellers for about six months.'

A man without roots and the dog who waited for him. Kate said, 'Sometimes, when you're away, would Baldy stay with me?'

'He might like that.'

'Where did he come from?'

'Beirut.'

She drew in a breath before she said, 'You're good with lame dogs.'

'Not particularly. Patience was never my strong suit.'

Her reporter's technique was helping her to sound calm and reasonable when what she really wanted to do was go over there and get so close that he would have to put his arms around her, and say, Talk to me about anything, or don't talk at all, I don't care, but please hold me.

'What did you tell Lawson Trout?' she asked.

'Nothing. He thought you'd taken the pictures along because they were local. He took it for granted you knew who I was, he thought the joke was on him.'

'Do you mind very much, me blowing your cover?'

Soon he would go off on his next assignment, but until then she very much wanted him to stay with her, and when he laughed and said, 'What the hell, what's it matter?' she laughed too, because that must mean a few days more.

The phone rang and she said, 'He's had time to get back to the office. It could be for you.'

People who knew him would start ringing Tad Brand, and when Mark stood up and said, 'Let's go,' Kate scurried for her coat and her bag.

Until now when they had eaten out she had mostly kept clear of places she had gone to with Alan. She had been scared of painful memories, but tonight it was as though years had passed since Alan Foster had been part of her life, and she said, 'I know where we'll go. It's on the canal, about five miles away. They do a good carvery and a super salad bowl.'

She and Mark shared a little table and concentrated on each other so that most of the time it seemed to Kate that nobody else was there. Leaving the restaurant, she passed the table she had occupied on her last visit, sitting opposite Alan listening to his talk about when they were married.

That was not much more than two months ago. He must have been involved with Celia then and cheating on Kate. But all she felt now was distaste, as if something underhand and unpleasant had happened to another girl a long time ago.

The phone was still ringing when they let themselves back into the house, although it was probably not the same caller. 'Let it ring,' said Mark.

'Can you do that?'

'Easy.'

It was late. She could walk upstairs and ignore it, and she said, 'I used to be good at shutting out what I didn't want to see or hear.'

'Hear no evil.' He touched her earlobes in a fingertip caress, then her temples. 'See no evil,' and as she looked at him she was afraid he would read her eyes and she turned towards the phone and reached for it.

'Kate? It's Alan,' said Alan.

She gave a croak that was almost laughter. 'Not about the letters again?'

'No—I know you didn't mean that. But I'm worried about you. This man you came back with from holiday—I've just heard who he is.'

The news had carried. If Tad Brand *had* been a serial killer it could hardly have spread faster. 'I've never met him myself, but he's got a rough reputation,' Alan was saying. 'I don't think you understand——'

'What do you mean, *rough*?' Beside her Mark, who had guessed the caller, grinned. Tough, she thought, but more a man of the world than you will ever be.

'I mean a hell-raiser, a womaniser.'

'Who could have told you he was a womaniser?' she enquired sweetly. 'Celia?' and she hung up while Alan was spluttering. 'That,' she said unnecessarily, 'was Alan.'

'I didn't think you were holding anyone else's letters. Am I the rough and randy character?'

'So he says. He's just heard who you are and he felt he should warn me.'

'Very considerate of him.'

'Ha!' said Kate. 'Are you a womaniser?'

'You should know.' Not with her, she wished he had been.

'Well,' she said lightly, 'that seems to be the rumour that's going around,' and Mark laughed.

'Trust a politician to get his facts wrong. Goodnight, Katy.'

She said goodnight and closed her bedroom door, and wondered if Denise knew where he was, if he had phoned Denise, met her even while he was here, and again she was lacerated with jealousy.

* * *

Next morning she needed no time at all to adjust to the idea of Mark being Tad Brand. The astonishing thing was that she had not suspected something of the sort. He could never be a nonentity. Of course he would be outstanding in whatever he did. She would have been happier for selfish reasons if he had been less well known, but it was easy to believe that his was a success story.

If she cared what others thought, bringing Tad Brand home with her was a brilliant move, nobody would be calling her poor Kate after that. But she didn't care. She had sloughed off the past, she was starting afresh, and over breakfast she asked, 'Are we still going to the cottage this weekend? Only now they know who you are you could get a better offer.'

'Do you want to go?' She nodded. 'Then we will.' And she wished she could take the day off work, because she wanted to be with him all the time.

The next best thing was walking together towards the studios and knowing he would be waiting for her tonight. This morning as they passed Ilse's boutique in the square Kate heard her name called and Ilse came hurrying out, grabbing Kate's arm and eyeing Mark. 'I never did get to meet——' she dropped her voice to a seductive purr, 'Tad, isn't it?' and Kate said,

'That's right, and this is Ilse.'

Mark was remembering the naming of the puppet—because Kate knew a cow called Ilse. His dark eyes gleamed with laughter as he said gravely, 'What a charming name.'

Ilse fluttered her lashes. 'Thank you. You missed my party, didn't you, but I'm not going to let you get away, so when will you come over? One evening next week?'

'I'll ring you,' Kate said firmly.

'Or shall I ring you?' said Ilse, still looking at Mark.

'Is she?' asked Mark as they walked away.

'Very much so,' said Kate.

He grinned. 'One cow called Ilse's enough, we'll give this one a miss.'

They reached Mark's car and Kate asked, 'Where are you going?'

'Looking up some friends.'

He had never said that before, but he must have like-minded colleagues and friends all over, and he could be tiring of just Kate for company.

'Will you come back or will you be staying the night with them?' She hoped she sounded casual. Before long he would stay with others, but please, not tonight.

'I'll be back,' he said. 'And don't forget the market in the morning. Don't leave your car here.'

'Not me,' she said. 'They don't write "Small but Sexy" on me twice.' He kissed her smiling lips and she went on smiling as she walked across the road and through the doors of Radio Danilo.

In the foyer Nicola caught up with her. 'Aren't you the dark horse?' said Nicola. 'No wonder you weren't letting anybody meet him!' She kept pace with Kate, going up the stairs. 'Did you know him before? You never just picked him up on holiday?'

'It was just how I told you.' Kate smiled a smug smile. 'Born lucky, aren't I?'

'You can say that again!' Nicola said emphatically and enviously, but Kate was not so sure. Meeting Mark and getting on so well with him was the best thing that had ever happened to her. Falling hopelessly for him could prove one of the toughest, but this morning she was the girl who had good reason to be smiling.

Most of her workmates knew Tad Brand by name. They were all in the media business and he was a top photographer and, like Lawson Trout, they presumed that Kate had been helping him keep a low profile. Well, it was out now and some of them had met him before, the news editor for one, who said, 'Give my best to Tad, tell him I'd like to have a drink with him.'

'I will,' Kate promised, and when she got another couple of messages she made notes and thought, I'm turning into a social secretary here.

She was busy all day. The run-up to Christmas had started and she was covering plans for the days ahead, in schools and stores, church fêtes, pantomime rehearsals. Mark would surely be gone before Christmas and she was going to miss him terribly, but he would be home tonight, and when work was through she got away as quickly as she could.

From Gina and George's wine bar across the square a photographer from the *Despatch* hailed her. 'Hey, Kate, hold on a minute!' When he reached her he said, 'By yourself? Where's Tad?'

'I don't know. He was meeting some friends.'

Harry Bush, who had a youngish face under grizzled grey hair, said, 'Remember me to him. We've worked together.'

'I'll tell him,' she said.

It had been lovely coming home and knowing that for the next twelve hours it was going to be just her and Mark. He was there before her tonight. Baldy came to meet her and Mark was in the kitchen, only a few steps away in the tiny house.

When she closed the front door she had shut out the rest of the world, but tonight she might as well have left the door wide open.

'I've got a page of messages for you,' she said. 'What I don't understand is why you weren't spotted before, because it seems that everybody I work with knows you.'

'I doubt that,' he said.

'How about Harry Bush and our news editor, Joe Murphy?'

'Yes.'

'You could have bumped into them any time.'

'I could have, but I didn't.' He had not been in town much and she had chosen out-of-the-way places when they had eaten out.

'Well, they know you're here now,' she said. 'And they all want to meet you.' She rummaged in her bag for her notebook. 'How does it feel to be famous?'

'To a limited audience. Here's a message for you.'

There was a torn sheet of paper on the hall table, that Trish had pushed through the letterbox earlier. 'We're just off,' Kate read. 'Taking all the food we'll need, so don't bother bringing anything but yourselves. See you tomorrow as soon as you can get away. P.S. Who the heck's Tad Brand?'

That made Kate smile, and Mark grinned and for a moment she was happy and safe, enclosed in a magic circle. But the circle broke within minutes. She had gone upstairs to change out of a skirt that had got splashed with poster paint this afternoon in a nursery school, when she heard the door knocker.

By the time she was into a pair of black trousers and had come out on to the landing the little hall below seemed crowded with the Tad Brand fan club. She wondered if the wine bar had emptied and they had all followed her up here, that wouldn't have pleased the proprietors. She saw Harry Bush, and a sound engineer from Radio Danilo who had sent a message to Tad, and Jenny and a few more, and as she walked downstairs Harry asked, 'All right, Kate? Don't mind us dropping in, do you?'

If Mark had wanted that she would have pleaded a prior engagement and got them out fairly quickly, but he looked pleased to see them, greeting some by name, being introduced to the rest as they all trooped through into the living-room.

'It was Harry's idea,' said Jenny. 'He said he was coming to see him and so did Tony, so we trailed along. 'I *say*, though, he is gorgeous!'

'The host with the most,' quipped Kate, accepting the unavoidable. 'Looks as if we're having a party.'

The impromptu get-together was a great success. Those who knew Tad were recalling when they'd met, trotting out names of friends and acquaintances. Stories were told and capped. They all seemed to be making themselves at home, and Kate, who was a hospitable girl although she would rather have had Mark to herself, went into the kitchen and started cutting sandwiches.

She handed these around and brought out a bottle of wine and sat on the floor, her back to the wall, her feet tucked in, watching her uninvited guests enjoying themselves.

Mark ... Tad ... did it. Even when he was sitting still he seemed to give out an electric current that was charging them up, and she had the weird sen-

sation that if he had left the room they would all
be switched off like a light going out.

They were in no hurry to leave. Jenny went first,
looking at her watch and wondering where the time
had gone. Then, slowly, most of the others. But a
hard core of men lingered until Kate wondered how
much longer they were staying.

She wished they would go or she would have no
time at all alone with Mark tonight. If he had been
her lover she could have turned to him, when the
last visitor left the house, and they could have made
up for the hours they had been kept apart. As it
was, there would be time for nothing, except to go
to her own bed and dream of tomorrow night, when
at last and gloriously she and Mark would be completely together.

She still had her packing to do, only an overnight
bag, but she could do that now. She went upstairs
and pulled her small suitcase from under the bed,
folding in oyster satin pyjamas and a change of
clothing for Sunday. She left it open for make-up
and toiletries, and caught herself yawning and
realised how tired she was.

She would hear when they were leaving and she
would go down, but until then she would relax on
the bed. Today had seen the end of her one-to-one
relationship with Mark. From now on outsiders
would be crowding in, some of them with stronger
claims on him than she had ever had.

But I love him, she thought, and it was the heart's
truth, filling her with such warmth and tenderness
that for a little while she felt safe and secure and
utterly content. Then the fantasy shattered, because he had said nothing about loving her. He liked
her, he would enjoy having her, but that was as far

as it went. And if she tried to explain how she felt
he was bound to wonder if discovering he was Tad
Brand was influencing her.

The last thing she was was star-struck, and she
wished now that she had admitted before that he
was like no other man she had ever met and she
was crazy about him.

A scrap of paper on the floor under the dressing-
table caught her eye, part of the letters she was
tearing up last night, and she got off the bed and
picked it up; it had a flashy 'A' on it that was Alan's
signing-off signature. She might as well finish
tearing them up, then she could dump them in the
dustbin.

There were still about half a dozen unripped, and
by coincidence the next one she took out of its envelope had been written just after that weekend at
Trish's cottage. Alan and Kate had gone up there
alone and Alan had not been very impressed, because the cottage was rugged, although the weather
had been glorious.

In this letter he said that being with her had more
than made up for the plumbing, and she remembered the cistern that used to flush itself in the night.
This was a longish letter, going overleaf, and she
read it walking round the room so that she was
standing by the window when the door opened and
Mark looked in to ask, 'Are you all right?'

'Of course.'

'What are you doing up here?'

'Waiting for them to go.' He could see the letter
in her hand, and when he said derisively,

'One of the famous letters? You're not still
reading them?' she made a hopeless move to hide
it, by ramming it into her trouser pocket. She did

that so jumpily that when she jerked her hand out the letter came with it and fell at her feet, and he picked it up in what seemed like slow motion.

Handing it to her, he read the opening line aloud—always the same until the last—'My own darling', and hearing Mark say that choked her. She had to gulp for air, and he said impatiently, 'If you still want the man, go and get him.'

'I *don't*.' She couldn't have got Alan back and she didn't want him, but she could understand how a man of action like Mark would have no patience with inaction.

'Then cut your losses and stop moping.' He thought she had come up here to read the letters, and she started to stammer, 'I——' but he was not listening, 'And if we're heading off for the Yorkshire Dales tomorrow,' he said, 'for goodness' sake cheer up. They're bleak enough this time of year. Go up there feeling depressed and you'll end with a nervous breakdown.'

'No, I won't,' she said.

'Glad to hear it. Are you coming down?'

'Are they staying the night? I think I'll go to bed.'

'Good idea.' He smiled suddenly. 'Go to sleep, Kate, and remember what you told me. Everything looks brighter in the morning.' She knew now the kind of memories that had been haunting him on the night of the storm, and she doubted if they had seemed brighter in the morning.

It was ironic, him thinking she was up here moping over Alan. Tomorrow she would make it clear that she was not depressed, and that their weekend together was going to be fantastic.

She was getting into bed when she heard them leaving and somebody shouted up the stairs,

''Night, Kate, see you in the morning.' She lay awake, although she was not expecting Mark to come to her room. Nor did he. When she heard his bedroom door close she sighed, and after a while she slept.

Breakfast was as usual, coffee and toast, taken walking around in Kate's case because they would be leaving as soon as she finished work. This afternoon, she hoped, later if she was delayed. She was packed, and leaving the house in order, so that she only had to collect her case and they could take Mark's car and head for the motorway.

He didn't walk with her to work this morning, and she dashed to the *Despatch* offices to get a newspaper. The pictures were on the front page and most of the stallholders had acquired a copy. 'Nice one of Ma Gear,' they called, waving papers at her, and when she got into the studios it was the same. They all had seen the photographs and they all thought they were magic, and Kate bathed a little in reflected glory, because Tad was brilliant and she was proud of him.

The trip to Yorkshire was general knowledge too. Somebody last night had asked Tad what he was doing on Sunday and been told that he and Kate were joining the Saunderses in their cottage. Kate was teased about that, but she didn't care. It was all friendly and, on the female side, usually envious. Good luck to you, everybody was saying.

'You went up there with Alan, didn't you?' Jenny recalled. 'I thought what he did was awful.' Then her big brown eyes glowed. 'But I'm so glad you've found somebody really super.'

I found him, Kate thought, I was lucky there, but keeping him is the problem. She was lucky again at lunchtime when the news editor told her there was nothing to keep her here, she could leave early for the weekend, and she almost, not quite, kissed him. Then she took off before anybody had second thoughts.

Mark was not at home, but he would be back before long. She brought her case down into the cottage and boiled the kettle for a quick coffee. She had the *Despatch* with her and she sat on the sofa to look at the pictures again and skim the rest of the news. Some of these stories might be followed up by radio interviews, local broadcasting and press often shared scoops, and she was wondering what she could do about a woman who said a flying saucer had landed in her orchard and taken off again when the phone rang for the first time.

It was a girl who knew that Alan had dumped Kate, and had just heard that the man who was staying with Kate was a big name and wanted some more details. Kate told her a few, then said that she had to go because they were off for the weekend, and when Esther asked, 'Where?' she said, 'Up north, goodbye for now,' and hung up.

The second call came almost as soon as she sat down again. 'Is Tad there?' a woman's voice asked, and Kate said insincerely,

'Sorry, no.'

'Tell him Denise rang.' You'll be lucky, Kate thought. 'All right, is he?'

'Fine.'

The woman was young and smiling, you could tell by the voice. 'He usually takes off between assignments to unwind. Kate, is it?'

'Yes.' Lots of people would know by now. He had been with friends yesterday, and she wondered what he had told them about her.

Denise was still smiling. 'You're the light relief this time, so have fun while it lasts.'

'I will,' said Kate. She didn't know who hung up first, but the phone was on its cradle and she was facing her own pale reflection in the oval wall mirror. You knew that, she told it. Your little highs and lows are keeping his mind off grimmer things for a while. No wonder he wasn't taking you up all the way to Yorkshire if you were likely to be gloomy all the time. So smile, girl, smile . . .

She smiled, a twitch of the lips at first, then wider to a beam that did look remarkably cheerful.

No one else rang, although it was over an hour before Mark returned, surprised to see her till she explained, 'I got off early. Ready?' There could be other calls any time, each one taking him a little further from her. When they came back they would be waiting, but once she was out of here and into his car no one could get at him till Monday morning.

He had brought a carrier bag in with him, full of goodies, although Trish had said there was no need for them to bring anything. They packed that in the car with their cases, and Baldy sprawled on the back seat while Kate climbed in beside Mark, and the car moved away leaving them all behind.

It was easy to act cheerful, because she was. They listened to local radio until they were out of range, and then they had music playing and she smiled whenever Mark looked at her. She chatted about the market traders and the photograph and described her morning amusingly. She made him smile and she had him laughing. He wanted good company, someone funny and bright, and Kate could be all of that.

Some time she would have to 'remember' that Denise had phoned, and that was all she needed to say. Not that Denise had told her she was the 'light relief', nor that she was determined to be the best and the brightest so that he would think of her fondly and want to be with her again. And never, ever, that she had read the letter in the glove compartment about the incredible weekend that Tad and Denise had spent together. Even in the car they were not really alone, not with that letter sitting there.

Kate gave directions with the help of a map towards the end, and at one crossroads reminisced, 'Last time we lost our way here.'

'We?' He had slowed down as she hesitated.

Now he turned to her and she said lightly, 'Alan was with me. He said it was my map reading, and I guess it was, because we ended up a mountain.'

'Happy days,' drawled Mark, and she said again, 'I guess,' because she had thought they were.

Simon's great-aunt's cottage had once been a small general store. The plain glass windows were large and a bell still rang over the front door. It opened on to the pavement, in grey stone with a grey slate roof, although red window frames and door brightened it.

As the car drew up the door opened and Simon and Trish came out with welcoming smiles. Bags were carried into the room that had been a shop, but was now furnished with comfortable old-fashioned bargains, and had a coal fire burning in the black-leaded grate.

Kate remembered Alan's dismay when he had stepped in here, and wondered how it was looking to Mark. Trish was saying, as if she didn't quite know how to handle this, 'Simon's been telling me you're a big shot.'

'Don't believe him,' said Mark, 'I'm not,' and Trish said,

'But you've got to be. Anyone who can make the twins look that good has got to be the best,' and everyone smiled, and after that it couldn't have been cosier.

Mark admired everything they had done here when they showed him around. They had worked hard, stripping down walls and woodwork, re-wiring and plastering, putting in fitted cupboards and shelves. The plumbing was next, as soon as they could afford it, and Mark's enthusiasm was genuine, and Trish whispered to Kate, 'Isn't he *nice*? Not a bit big-headed, is he? And Simon says he's famous.'

There's no conceit in him, thought Kate, but he knows his worth. He is his own man, and that's the trouble, because I want him to be mine.

When their cases were put beside the bed she would be sharing with Mark she couldn't look at him, and she said quickly, 'I don't know what's in the carrier, but shouldn't we be opening it?' and led the way downstairs to the kitchen table, where the bag spilled out some delicious edibles and a couple of bottles that Simon drooled over.

Trish had a meal ready, and it turned into a feast, with them all sitting round the glowing fire and Kate being the life and soul of the party. She felt good, she really did, and when they started discussing where they would go tomorrow she said, 'The

Trough of Roland is beautiful, but it could be chilly this time of year. When I went it was hot, the sun was shining . . .' Her voice trailed and everybody knew she was talking about her summer stay with the man who had thrown her over for another girl. She would have gone on to babble something to fill the silence, but Trish leaned forward and said earnestly,

'Oh, Kate, it's lovely to see you so happy,' and Kate trilled with laughter.

'Of course I'm happy. Aren't we all? Good food, good friends, and with any luck at all good weather in the morning.'

She sounded shrill, but Simon and Trish didn't notice. They went on with their suggestions for tomorrow, and Kate nodded and smiled and felt Mark watching her with dark speculative eyes.

There was a limit to gaiety. She would have enjoyed the ride up here and this get-together with Trish and Simon, and she desperately wanted to sleep with Mark tonight. But she had hyped herself up after that phone call, playing the role of good companion with no let-up until she felt like an actress when the curtain was falling, still smiling and animated but drained and empty inside.

Bedtime needed organising. Hot water bottles had to be filled, because there was no heating up there and away from the fire it was chilly. The girls took the bathroom first, and Kate got into her satin pyjamas and sat with blankets and eiderdown up to her chin, hugging one bottle and with her feet on the other.

Last time there had been a heatwave so that even a sheet had seemed oppressive. Last time she had been alone in the house with Alan. Tonight she could hear the men downstairs, doors opening and closing.

This was a pretty room, with pink rosebuds on the wallpaper and curtains, and so small that the low-watt bulb lit it brightly, and when Mark came in, wearing dark pyjama trousers, bare-footed, bare-chested, his tanned skin gleamed like bronze.

He put the clothes he was carrying on a chair and Kate asked, 'Where's Baldy?'

'By the fire. We came to an arrangement.'

'Doesn't he approve of ladies in your bed?' she teased, but a pulse was beating, tightening her throat.

'It's a question of space.'

It was a big old-fashioned brass-knobbed bed, and she glanced down at the pillow beside her. When Alan had been with her she had thought she would die for him, but now she could hardly remember what he looked like. She began to chatter, 'The water bottles take most of the room. It's like being on a water bed. Only I never have, have you?'

'No.' Mark turned out the light and drew back the curtains. Silhouetted for a moment in the window and then a dark shadow coming towards her, and a lean hard body lowered on to the bed.

She was sitting up still, shaking with the violence of her own heartbeats, as he put an arm around her, drawing her to him. She went awkwardly, bumping her nose on his collarbone, then breathing in the faintly musky male warmth of his damp skin.

It was the most erotic aroma she had ever encountered, a slow and sensuous foreplay on her senses, so that she relaxed as the warmth began to tingle in her own blood. He stroked her hair gently and the rhythmic touch ran throbbing through her

veins until her head fell back and she lay with closed
eyes in the circle of his arms.

His next, more intimate move would have triggered a rapturous response, and at first she thought
the clamour was the hammering of her heart. Only
for a few seconds, of course, because Mark was
saying, 'What the hell is that?' and it was Trish and
Simon's antique plumbing thundering out a midnight sonata.

Downstairs Baldy was barking, and Simon
shouted, 'Sorry about this!'

'It's the plumbing,' said Kate. 'It gets airlocks.
Last time I was here it went off about two in the
morning and we nearly fell out of bed.'

She wished she had not said that, and a giggle
she couldn't contain bubbled up into laughter and
Mark said drily, 'It isn't that funny.'

She clapped a hand across her mouth because
this was not laughter, it was nearer hysteria, and
when he said, 'We shouldn't have come here,' she
shivered and waited until the pipes and the dog were
quietening down before she asked,

'Why not?'

'Because Trish is wrong—you're not happy.
You've been on a nervous high ever since we set
out. Talking non-stop got you through the day.' His
arm lay light on her shoulders and he sounded cynically amused. 'How were you getting through the
night in this bed? By closing your eyes and thinking
of Alan?'

'*No*!' Kate shook her head, her facial muscles
clenching, and he lifted her chin so that she was
staring up at him and asked her, 'Am I always going
to have trouble getting you to look at me?' His eyes
seemed darker than the shadows, she could read

nothing there, but his touch had been tender and would have been passionate, and she begged,

'Please make love to me.'

'On the whole I don't think that would be a good idea.'

He could have been turning down a drink, and she lashed out, 'You could always think of Denise!' and when one of his eyebrows arched slightly she muttered, 'There was a phone call just before we left. I'm sorry, I forgot.'

He seemed to believe her. He said, 'But of course you had other things on your mind,' as if she had been thinking of Alan and there was no room for anything else.

The clanging pipes were silent now. Baldy had decided the intruder had been routed and the night was quiet. 'Go to sleep,' said Mark. He lay down himself, arms clasped behind his head. 'They're going to have us traipsing for miles tomorrow.'

She couldn't sleep beside him like this, but she had managed to ruin everything for tonight, maybe for ever. She turned on her side, her face averted, silent tears sliding down her cheeks, breathing steadily so that he would think she slept until at last she did.

CHAPTER EIGHT

WHEN Kate awoke she was alone and it was broad daylight. Others were up. She could smell bacon frying and felt faintly nauseous.

How could she have slept so heavily that Mark could slip out of bed and get himself and his clothes out of the room? He was a quiet mover, and he probably had had practice in early and silent retreats, but it was not a good start to the day. She would much rather have woken him and lain drowsily together for a few minutes, slowly talking themselves awake.

Well, she was awake now, and her first meeting with Mark would be in front of Simon and Trish. No chance of saying, 'I wasn't thinking about Alan yesterday. Why should I, when the only man on my mind is you?'

She tied the waist girdle of her robe and went downstairs—the lino was cold to her bare feet—to the door that opened into the kitchen. Trish was at the gas stove with a frying pan, Simon was at the table with a guide book, and both beamed at her as she stood tousle-haired in the doorway. There was no sign of Mark or Baldy, and Trish enquired archly, 'Sleep well?'

'After the pipes shut up,' said Simon.

'Er—yes, thank you.' Kate could feel herself blushing and knew how they were interpreting that, and asked quickly,

'Where's Mark?'

'Walking the dog,' said Trish.

Kate, wondering if he was also phoning Denise, said, 'I'd better get dressed,' and went back upstairs.

She was not at her best, in spite of touches of colour on lips and cheekbones and a flick of mascara. Her hair shone and her smile could be bright, but she had a rival who was so sure of Tad-as-she-called-him that any other girl was a joke. Almost surely he was talking to Denise now, while Kate dressed for a day's trekking over the Dales and felt downright drab.

They had returned when she came down. Baldy wagged his tail and Mark's smile reached her like a caress, light and sweet. 'You should have woken me,' she said.

'I hadn't the heart. You looked so comfortable.' He put an arm around her and she thought, now I am comfortable.

'We thought we'd do the lead mining trail,' Simon told her. 'And take in the old Corpse Way—do you know it?'

'No,' she said, 'but it sounds a load of laughs.'

As it happened, it was. They had a super day. The remains of the old mines were fascinating, and they walked the narrow road down which the dwellers in the hills had carried their dead to the church in the valley, and the Dales were beautiful. They picnicked from a hamper in the car, and ended with a meal in a seventeenth century inn before they drove back to the cottage.

In the car Trish said, 'Thanks for staying with us. I'm sure you'd rather have been on your own, but being with you has made this one of our best days ever up here.'

Kate could believe that, because everything was better when Mark was around. His energy and humour were infectious, so that Simon and Trish had been in high spirits and very good company themselves all day long. Kate had enjoyed herself too, although she was always aware of the dangerously complex man behind the easy charm.

'Thank you, both of you,' Mark was saying now.

'Any time you want to get away on your own,' said Simon, 'the cottage is here.'

Mark thanked him again. 'You're welcome to the tower,' he said. 'Kate could give you directions. But I can't say how long for, I've just had an offer for it.'

It had to be recently, and why *should* he tell her right away? It was none of her business. But it meant that she would never go there again, and she held down a sigh and said, 'A good offer?'

'Yes,' said Mark.

'That's good,' said Kate, and looked out at the hedgerows rushing past the car and thought that time seemed to be hurtling her on at the same dizzy rate and getting her nowhere.

But the working hours on Monday dragged by. She had not had much sleep the night before, but only because Trish and Simon were driving back overnight as Simon had to be at work by half-past eight; and as Kate was due in at nine it made sense that she and Mark should leave at the same time. So they drank coffee and talked into the early hours and then drove back, and the only bed Kate had crawled into last night had been her own bed in her own house.

In the office everyone believed her when she said she had had a wonderful time and, as far as it went, she had; but nothing had quite gone the way she'd hoped and time was running out. Mark was not involved enough to make any sort of claim, and unless she could find the nerve to declare outright that she was crazy for him he would be leaving and she would be left with enough frustration and regret to warp all the happy memories.

It would not have surprised her to find company waiting when she got home from work on Monday, but no sooner had it registered that Mark was alone than he was telling her, 'I've just accepted an invitation for tonight, and I'd like you to come with me.'

Of course, she thought wearily. So long as you're here there'll always be somebody wanting the pleasure of your company. 'Where?' she asked.

'Clifford Chambers rang. He has a few friends in.' That meant Celia and probably Alan. Mark was watching her closely, and she gave a small shrug and asked, 'Do you know him well?'

'We've met, at official functions mostly.'

'And they both want to see you again.' He'd accepted, so he must want to see them. 'What time?'

'As soon as we can get along.'

'Give me a few minutes,' and she hurried upstairs.

Only a few days ago the prospect of facing Alan and Celia together had reduced her to jelly. She didn't want to go to the Chamberses' home tonight, but she wasn't dreading it. She would have felt the same about anybody who was using up her time with Mark. That they were a thumping nuisance, but that was all. She rushed through a repair job on her appearance because the sooner they arrived, the sooner they might get away.

She had never before been invited through the gates in the high white walls, on a hillside just outside the town, but she knew where Clifford Chambers and his daughter lived. The gates were open and lights were on in most of the mullioned white-shuttered windows as Mark drew up in the broad gravelled courtyard that fronted the house.

A soberly clad woman opened the door and Clifford Chambers himself was coming up behind her. With his smooth silvered hair, patrician, slightly florid features and confident manner, he looked what he was, an elder statesman whose words still carried weight.

Kate knew he could be a pompous chauvinist, but, with a friendly hand on the younger man's shoulders, his welcome for Mark was warm. 'Tad m'boy, how long have you been in town? I only heard today you were here.' His well-preserved smile switched to Kate. 'Come in,' he said effusively, 'come in.'

They were already in the house, but he meant the drawing-room, and before they could get down the long hall Celia had stepped out, stood for a second, then came running and squealing towards them.

'I couldn't *believe* it!' If her father's welcome had been cordial hers was ecstatic. 'I told Daddy he had to get you round right away before you vanished again.' She had slipped a hand through Mark's arm and was looking up at him, her pretty doll face wreathed in smiles. 'I didn't know you knew—er—Kate,' she said. 'But then you know everybody, don't you?'

'That's the media business for you,' Kate drawled. 'We cover the world.' Mark grinned across at her, but Celia didn't seem to hear, and the Chamberses ushered their guests into their elegant drawing-room.

Kate got an immediate impression of gracious living, but she was watching Celia with Mark, so that it was a few moments before she even noticed that Alan was not here. The two men, sitting with drinks beside them, were from Clifford Chambers' inner circle. Kate knew them slightly, and the wives with them, and they all smiled briefly at her and greeted Tad Brand—who was top of his league with an award-winning talent—as one of their own. They were delighted to meet him, while Kate, sitting with a dry sherry, was almost ignored.

She told herself that was not bothering her because this was as good as a play; and she sat back, slim legs crossed, fingering the stem of her glass, watching the performance.

Tad was the star. All the talk and attention was centred on him, and he handled it like a professional. Listening and watching, Kate felt she knew the tricks he was using to charm the company, especially Celia, whose eyes lit eagerly every time he turned to her.

But she's so shallow, thought Kate, pampered and cute and *stupid*, so why are you taken with her? And the rest of them bore you, so what are we doing here, why did you say you'd come?

Celia was well on the way to a king-size crush on him, and that had to be flattering, although Kate would not have thought Mark was susceptible to flattery.

But Celia was so pretty, bouncing off her chair with excitement, and Kate began to wonder if Alan's main attraction might have been the secrecy of their affair. Now everything was in the open the thrill might have gone out of it for Celia.

Tad Brand was excitement personified, but if she had ideas of trading Alan in for him she was going to get slapped down so hard that she could be seeing stars for a long, long time. Fury rose in Kate and her fingers tightened, white-knuckled, round her glass. She put that down quickly before she broke it, and Celia's voice reached her through a ringing in her ears. She felt like a time-bomb about to explode. 'You will be here for the Press Ball, won't you?' Celia was cooing. 'The Press Ball's always such fun. Next week, isn't it?'

This was the first time she had addressed Kate, almost the first time anyone had. Kate said, 'A week on Friday,' and Mark said,

'I may be here.' Then he glanced at his watch. 'Now I'm afraid we must be going. It's been a pleasure.'

Has it not? Kate thought sourly, and she was on her feet at once.

They were seen out with great affability. Well, Tad was. Kate was included because she was with him, but when someone said, 'We hope to see you again,' that didn't mean Kate.

On their way back Mark turned on the car radio and Kate pretended to listen to one of her colleagues because she couldn't trust herself to speak. A few more minutes and she would have asked where Alan was, and had Celia tried on his grandmother's ring yet?

She would have made a fool of herself, but jealousy was ripping her up, and when she turned the key in her front door she hurried ahead upstairs. 'Hang on,' said Mark. 'They weren't that boring.'

She stopped at the top as he followed her and they faced each other on the narrow landing. '*Boring*?' she shrilled. 'Celia wasn't boring, she was scintillating!' Now she couldn't shut up. 'Well worth turning up for, was Celia. It was her you wanted to see again, of course.'

'No,' he said. 'I wanted to see Alan Foster. It seemed time that I met the man.'

'Oh.'

'And I might be able to help you there.' Arms folded, eyes glittering under dark brows, he looked like the devil again. 'It wouldn't be hard to change Celia Chambers' mind, such as it is, about Alan Foster or anything else. Would you like that to happen? How about this Press Ball? Do you want a public announcement?'

He could do that. Celia would leave Alan for him. It would be sadistic and cold-blooded, unless he was prepared for an affair with Celia, and that was impossible. She put her hands to burning cheeks and shrieked, '*No!*'

'If you don't want that, what do you want?' Somehow his fingers were wound in her hair, pulling her head back, and his voice was soft and savage. 'He's still on your mind. You're still reading his letters, taking him with you up to the cottage, and into our bed.'

She cried out, 'I wasn't thinking of Alan. I was——' she gulped and began to gabble. 'It was your phone call. Denise said you always took off between assignments to unwind, and I was your escapism this time, taking your mind off things. I was trying——' she gulped again '—trying to keep you amused.'

'Well, it didn't work.' His voice was ragged now. 'For your information, your relaxation value is nil. I'm going out of my mind over you.' He looked haggard, desperate, and the words spoke themselves.

'I love you.'

'What?'

She couldn't look away from the dazzling directness of his eyes. She said, 'All along, I think. Not like Alan. Not like anybody or anything else that's ever happened to me. That's why I was scared to look at you, because you'd see how I was feeling and tell me it couldn't make sense. Not so quickly, so completely.'

The hands in her hair had gentled, cradling her face. 'It makes sense,' he said huskily. 'Every step of the way from the beginning, because it's how I feel.' She could hear the beating of her heart, his heart. 'Oh, Katy,' he said, and folded strong arms around her, holding her to him.

She couldn't stop looking into his eyes. She put her arms around his waist and hugged hard, and the closeness and hardness of him reached her through the barrier of clothing. Her fingers, or his, undid the buttons of her coat. It fell as they moved through the open door towards the bed, stripping somehow but never, it seemed to Kate, breaking the eye-contact, as though they had found each other at last and could not bear to look away.

Kicking off shoes, leaving a trail of clothing, she slid between cold sheets, and he moved with her, his breath on her lips. It was almost dark in here, but she could see every plane and hollow of his face, and she knew the body that was naked against hers as if it was part of her and only together were they whole.

Their lovemaking was a singing ecstasy, from the murmuring joy of Mark's fingers brushing the nape of her neck to the unbelievable crescendo of her lover within her and every throbbing nerve welcoming and holding him. She screamed in tune with that, then floated gently down while the music played on, happier and safer than she had ever been before.

She was lying in the warm circle of his arms, fitting so snugly that it made her smile. She looked up, opening her eyes but not moving her head, and he smiled at her and said, 'Hello, my love.'

'You wouldn't be snoring?'

'Hardly.'

It was Baldy, of course, sound asleep on the rug beside the bed, and she asked, 'Did he sleep all through—well, you know?'

'I wouldn't know. There could have been a pack of wolves howling in here and I wouldn't have noticed. He probably went to sleep about the same time you did.'

'I went to sleep?' It had been the loveliest rest and the best of all awakenings. She couldn't be jealous of anyone any more, but she heard herself asking, 'Was there Celia?'

'Certainly not.'

'But there was Denise.' And others.

'Like there was Alan.' Which meant they were history, and a moment later, 'You'd better marry me.'

'Are you joking?'

'Look at me, Katy.' She could see his soul in his eyes, and it took her breath away that he should care so much for her so that she could only stammer,

'Why?'

He grinned, and she started smiling again when he said, 'Because if you don't I shall fix it that your car gets parked in the square every Friday night. I'm a dirty fighter.'

'I believe that.' She rested her cheek on his shoulder and breathed in. 'But you're a lovely lover, and you smell so good.'

'I'm addicted to you too, so tell me how I'm going to manage without you even with my ring on your finger?' She would hate the partings, but she wouldn't think about them now. Then he said, 'Sometimes you could come with me.'

Of course she could. She was a journalist, she could work with him. '*Yes*,' she said. 'You've got your very own Hetty; I'll turn up everywhere.'

Home was where he was, her life was where he was. 'I suppose,' she said, 'you're selling the tower?'

'Don't you want me to?'

'I'd like to go back. Doesn't it earn its keep in holiday lets?'

'You were the first. My friends use it, I use it. But I wanted you to stay. As I told you—right from the beginning.' He looked down at her, lying in the crook of his arm. 'If you want it,' he said, 'make me an offer.'

Kate pulled a face. 'Me? I'm only a working girl who's about to chuck in her job to go swanning around the world.'

'We're not talking cash here.'

'Oh!' Her eyes lit with laughter and love. 'In that case.' She reached up to pull him down and just before she kissed his mouth he said,

'It's yours.'